Praise for EDGES ("THE FRAGILE MISTRESS")

"In Edges Leora Smith skillfully tells the story of a girl of fourteen in the wake of her father's suicide, brought abruptly by her distraught mother from a comfortable suburban Westchester to the harsh terrain of a young State of Israel. The girl is caught in the maelstrom of political claims between Israel and a West Bank, still part of the Kingdom of Jordan. The turmoil both of the girl and her mother is graphically detailed as they struggle to define themselves in the light of a haunted past and present. The poetry of the girl's sexual awakening ripples through many pages, softening the fierce realities of the conflict between Arab and Jew. The pages evoke as well the memories of a shared land, and the mother's childhood growing up in an old Jerusalem before the city was separated by physical barriers, the religious, cultural, divide between Arab and Jew easier to bridge. The author's vivid sense of landscape, her gift for identifying with both mother and daughter, Arab and Jew, gives the novel a unique sense of balance and brings the reader, regardless of political conviction into sympathy with this portrait of a vanished Jerusalem."

—MARK MIRSKY, AUTHOR, EDITOR, "FICTION"

I0525092

"A feverish, sensual, remarkable book."

—MEREDITH SUE WILLIS

"Edges" is a dark and penetrating look at pre-1967 Israel and Palestine through the eyes of a 14 year old Liana Barish. After her American father's suicide, Liana's Jerusalem-born mother decides to take Liana and her sister back to her homeland, where her family had lived for four generations. Once they get to Israel Liana, who feels overwhelmed and suffocated by her mother, begins to detach herself from her. She embarks on a mission of self-discovery to learn why her mother does not speak about her father and why he took his own life. Edges is well-written, powerful in both imagery and subject matter . . ."

— "JEWISH BOOK WORLD", SPRING 2006

"Edges is an elegantly written, quite moving novel that has a lot to say about love, identity, history and the meaning of nationality. The book is worth reading alone for its superb language, but it is gripping and unforgettable as well in its story telling and evocation of place and emotions. It is a wonderful novel by an author with a quite accomplished voice and style, one well deserving a wide and receptive audience.

—Oscar Hijuelos, author of the Pulitzer-prize winning novel, *The Mambo King Sings Songs Of Love*

"Edges is an elegant and moving novel. Leora Skolkin-Smith has that rare gift of the writer who can convey the sensibilit —the essence of a place and its people—with precision and clarity. A provocative debut."

—Katharine Weber, author of *Triangle, Little Women, The Music Lesson*

"Where, and how and to whom do we really belong? Skolkin's brilliant debut novel is a hypnotic meditation on the ever-changing boundaries of love and need. A coming of age story of the bond between a young American and her powerful mother, etched in a wartime Mideast as shifting and dangerous and mysterious as the Israeli desert."

—Caroline Leavitt, author of *Girls In Trouble, Coming Back To Me,* and *Breathe*

"EDGES is a novel told with restraint and poetic precision...memorable (for the) the sense of place that Ms. Skolkin-Smith has achieved—the sunny and scary Jerusalem and countryside—and the hope, love, hate and fatalism of the groups, Palestinian and Israeli, living amongst and apart from each other..."

—Robert Whitcomb, "The Providence Journal"

"With EDGES, Leora Skolkin-Smith earns her place among the most gifted of contemporary American authors. The novel is a reminder that works of fiction can offer the depth, color, texture, passion of a fine painting and a great symphony. This is more than a coming-of-age story; it is a powerful and beautifully wrought account of passion and hope for a girl and for a country."

—Victoria Zackheim, Author, *The Bone Weaver* , Editor of Anthologies *The Other Woman,* and *For Keeps*

"When Liana Bialik's mother takes her from the predictable confines of Westchester County, New York, to Israel in the middle of the 1960s' conflicts, Liana's worldview and her sense of self are transformed. Heat; dust; the mingled scents of food, flowers, people, spice markets; simmering tensions between Israelis and Palestinians; and in the middle, a 14-year-old on the cusp of womanhood. Leora Skolkin-Smith has written a passionate, richly atmospheric novel whose intimacy reads like a memoir. The mother's longing for the Palestine of old; Liana's edgy girl-woman voice; the mistrustful bargaining of a Palestinian shopkeeper. It's all here, and it's terrific."
— A.C.S. ••• © AudioFile 2008
WINNER OF EARPHONES AWARD FOR ORIGINAL AUDIOBOOK, MIDSUMMER SOUND COMPANY, 2007

"This is an intimate and compelling portrait of ordinary people caught in an extraordinary time and place. This first publication from Glad Day Books, Grace Paley's new imprint, is a promising debut."
—*Robert Gray, author of Publisher's Marketplace and Fresh Eyes*

"Ms. Skolkin-Smith's first novel is a captivating story giving the reader a view into a land and culture of another time...This slim novel has wonderful images and evocative writing. It is a novel about coming-of-age and about family and love. I imagine it is one that will stay with me for a long time."
—"BOOKGIRL NIGHTSTAND"

"Identity was never so hard-won as Liana's...somehow I felt I did understand Israel and as a country as much as a homeland. I could smell the land and feel the heat and the dust as well as the perils...The writing is spontaneous and fresh and the dialogue crafted with such a natural feel that you hear it as you read...A small enough book to pass by next to all those might tomes shouting read me, but one to seek out and savour for sure.. It's been a vibrant and welcoming introduction as I set foot in Israel from my armchair..."
—LYNNE HATWELL, "Dovegrey Scribbles"

The
Fragile
Mistress

By Leora Skolkin-Smith

H\S
Hamilton Stone Editions
Maplewood, New Jersey

The Fragile Mistress is an expanded edition of the work originally published under the title *Edges*.

Skolkin-Smith, Leora, 1952-
 The fragile mistress / by Leora Skolkin-Smith.
 p. cm.
 Based on: Edges.
 ISBN 978-0-9801786-4-7 (alk. paper)
 1. Jewish girls—Fiction. 2. Jewish families—Jerusalem—Fiction. 3. Jerusalem—Fiction. 4. Israel—Fiction. 5. Jewish fiction. I. Skolkin-Smith, Leora, 1952- Edges. II. Title.
 PS3619.K65F73 2010
 813'.6--dc22
     2009021395

Hamilton Stone Editions,
P.O. Box 43, Maplewood NJ 07040
Printed in the USA

Acknowledgments

The author would like to thank the friends and companions without whom this novel could never have been brought into life: her husband, Matthew Smith, Mervyn Peskin, Caroline Leavitt, Robert Nichols and Grace Paley.

Dedication

For my mother, Rachel Silberstein Skolkin,
and for all the family here and there.

The
Fragile
Mistress

. . . *It was said in the Talmud that the daughters of Zion were haughty and walked with necks stretched like spears and eyes painted with sikra (red dye). When Isaiah was asked by God:*

"What are these women doing here? They must be banished hence! "Isaiah told the women: "Vow penitence so that Israel's foes do not come at you! "But the women replied: "What if Israel's foes do come, what can they possibly do to us? An officer will see me and take me as a lover, a prefect will see me and take me as his wife, and a general will see me, take me, and seat me in his carriage.

. . . *I am only a mistress and therefore have no foes . . .*

—AN OLD JEWISH FABLE

1

THAT SUMMER IN 1963, the government of Jordan granted the few Israeli descendants of old Jerusalem permission to dig up a gravesite in the Arab territories and transport the souls and skeletons of their lost ones to Israel's side of the border.

My mother, my sister, Ivy and I sat on a packed El Al plane on our way to Jerusalem from our home in America, to participate in a burial ceremony for an uncle I had never met.

I flicked on the passenger light above my head. By my wristwatch it was only three-thirty-seven p.m., New York time, but, when I gazed out the plane window, the sky was full of coal-like clouds.

"Want some chocolate?" My mother held an 18-ounce duty-free bar of Hershey's almond chocolate under my nose. "It's seven more hours until we reach Tel Aviv, will you survive?"

"No," I said.

Dot Elizar had been buried, my mother said, in the mixed cemetery among the Arab and Jewish war heroes before the War of Independence divided the city. Now he would be dug up and reburied in the new Jerusalem. The Ceremony of the Graves was to take place near the President's House.

Why should I have cared about my uncle Elizar? For many years, we had not visited Israel, though my mother had grown up there, in the rugged and hot geography of what was known in the 1930s as: Palestine. I remembered only vaguely going there as a baby, its hot sun, and my mother's childhood house on a limestone street behind some eucalyptus trees.

I was fourteen years old, and it was two years after my father's suicide. My mother planned for a long stay in Jerusalem.

My mother had never spoken about her brother Elizar or old Jerusalem. The faces of World War II's displaced persons, and their refugee boats on the Mediterranean Sea did not appear in the same photographs my mother showed me of herself in Palestine. A playful little girl with short red hair, wearing boy's khaki shorts and hiking boots. The rest of my mother's history I had put together loosely from other pictures she kept in the basement of our Northern Westchester home— glimpses of letters and more photographs of my mother, Ada Silberfeld, the bigheaded woman, hugging the cedars trees of Abu Tor during the bombings and shellings that shook the quiet streets of Jerusalem by 1946. She had married my father, an American, after coming over to New York Harbor with a chaperone, on a War Brides ship from Haifa.

Now she separated the chocolate squares into chunky shards with her stubby fingers, pushing pieces at the back of her mouth, and making a loud sucking noise.

"The travel agent was such an idiot," she said, pulling at her tent dress. Her legs were bare, and her summer jacket was on backwards, the Bonwit Teller label glistening in the soft plane light. "But, she did tell me we will land somewhere in Europe for a few hours, for the plane to get more fuel."

"In Paris?" I asked.

"Paris? Why Paris? No, I am sure it will be in Switzerland. It will not even be worth it to get off the airplane, Liana. But, maybe they will have some good Swiss chocolate on the plane for a change. That is if the stewardesses get off to go make pee-pee in the airport there."

"Oh." I let the airplane magazine I had on my lap slide to the floor with the unspoken embarrassment I felt sitting next to her.

We had been in the air for several hours, and the outside atmosphere was changing into a velvety cloak of black and white. The odor of fresh almonds and hardened cocoa from my mother's chocolate permeated the enclosed air, as if the bar were breathing, exhaling a warm, luscious scent.

"What's the matter, Liana?" My mother licked her upper lip with her browned tongue and then folded the silver foil over the remaining chocolate in her hand. "Talk to me darling," she said.

Her kindness pained me. I wished I could return it, but I couldn't. I wished I was happy about it, but I wasn't. I did not want her attention. I had come to prefer her neglecting me, demanding nothing of me but to show up when she thought something she did—like preparing dinner for Ivy and me that night, or asking me once if I needed some fresh bath towels—might be as important as it was, before.

The splinters of chocolate had settled on her chest as if they were the jewelry pieces meant to go with her loose outfit and manners. "Aren't we stopping off somewhere else?" I asked.

"Look Liana," my mother whispered into my ear. "We will not tell anyone in Israel about the accident."

Some time after midnight on a mild summer night, my father had catapulted off a country road in Katonah in his blue MG sports car, crashing into the woods. There had been letters back and forth between my father and his former psychiatrist which, found, proved he had been thinking about ending his life, of letting go of the ivory steering wheel of his MG just that way. It had all been like some premeditated murder on Perry Mason.

On the airplane wall, by the entrance towards the pilot and his cockpit, was a clock like they had in my junior high school. The giant utility of timekeeping made me think about the days to come, how slow they would go.

The lights inside the plane dimmed to signal the approach of night.

Silhouetted against the shiny sides of the coach in the first four rows of seats were a group of dark-suited Hasidic men and their families. Their curly black beards and side locks made them look like shadowed rag dolls. Six or seven crates of their duty-free Smirvoff vodka bottles were stashed under their seats. In 1963, the plane cabins were small and packed with as many duty-free articles from the airport store as passengers could carry on with them. Chocolate, laundry detergent, Winston cigarette cartons and other untaxed items from Idlewild airport cluttered the plane. I studied the Hasidic men. Too fatherly, their bodies so close, like it was with my mother. A nightmare of fathers in the wrong attire. They bobbed and jiggled and splashed their messy outbursts of affection onto their make-upless wives, their pale children. The vodka and their full laughter—where were we going? To what world before? It was completely without my father. And had nothing to do with Ivy or me.

I looked around my mother at my sister seated in the opposite aisle seat. After my father's funeral, Ivy had started collecting records of incantations from India or Africa, with record jackets on which cameo pictures of spiritual amulets and naked black Warriors would appear. She also made notations onto little index cards she took from the high school library stack about the Amish who lived in some of the colonial farmhouses further down the road from us. She put a motto up on her bedroom wall in Westchester which read: "The Amish people live kindly and decently. They love what is . . . and are joyful." She had already tried marijuana and knew the places in the woods in Katonah we could take some six packs of Colt 45 malt liquor, and consider the all-embracing energy waves of nature. We drank nips of Southern Comfort, too, in the cold, raking through the Westchester snowdrifts in large rubber boots where sometimes the rocks were stained with deer blood, fallen fragile and beautiful animals. We had searched for hunter's tracks, to find enemies. We had to be careful about how we moved about now, Ivy had said, and about what we said, about what secret thoughts swam in our brains, in case it had been our bad spiritual vibrations that had made my father leave us, or that had made him do what he did.

Now Ivy was sipping from a container of Tropicana orange juice she bought at the duty-free shop while we waited for our flight.

Ivy was sixteen. She was taller than me, with long, chestnut hair and a thin, difficult face—small-eyed and sharp. Her long body gave off the odor of cigarettes and soap. My moods were as changeable and labile as my mother's, they darkened or lightened. Ivy often prided herself on not being one of us at all and could easily establish her emotional residence elsewhere.

Once my mother was safe again, with her first family, and if I planned it right, I could find a way to leave. I would find the places my father told me about in Paris. I could wire back to my sister, and she could come, too. I will enjoy that, I thought, pulling my sister out with me. Somehow, I thought I would stay in Israel for only as long as it took me to find enough money to get to Paris, to what I knew of the famous streets that could be described in the large, sensual words Marcel Proust had brought my father and me when I was still too young to understand what they meant. Lyrical overtures about the loveless and abandoned. I had no knowledge of airfares, but I believed the situation, all of us being in Israel, once the plane landed, could be undone if I acted forcefully enough.

After my father's "accident," my mother could not recognize herself in the picture of her life. If the white drifts on the ground were tall and thick, she would let me stay home from school. She lay silent in the house in Katonah, ringing her hands under her bed sheets, stunned and outraged as if it were just at that moment that she heard the news of my father's death. And then, she would look at me, look appealingly to me. She grew more careless about herself as time went on. Her body was usually without undergarments which gave the sheets a hot, wettish odor. Her hair and face creams gave off a strong, fruity smell and tempered the raw coarse aromas that got loose from her flesh. And then, her strength appeared more muscular in its war against grief and distress than I had ever seen it. I wanted to be near it. Sometimes I stayed home from school, and she took me into bed with her. We watched television in her bed together: "Our Miss Brooks" and "The

Many Loves of Dobie Gillis," "Queen for A Day." We watched a chimpanzee at Cape Canaveral complete his one day space flight towards the moon. I believed I knew what we were doing together those long, housebound mornings and afternoons. We were preparing for the possibility that there would never be another man in our lives, that we better get used to it being just us.

"Look." My mother adjusted herself in her seat, reached into the left pocket of her tent dress and whisked out an envelope my aunt had sent her from One Metaduleh Street. She pulled out three recent photographs, fanning them out with her fingers like a trick deck of cards and holding them in front of my eyes. There was Jerusalem, "The Border Confused City," the 1963 *Life* magazine article called it. My mother had left the article on my bedroom bureau in Katonah. "In a Pentateuchal sense of the word," said the article I read that night two weeks ago, "Jerusalem is a geography that is everywhere a matter of more or less chaos, looking still like a Biblical place where the sea had not yet separated from the sky and the land was not yet."

I had looked up "Pentateuchal" in the dictionary and had not even found a definition for that.

Now I stared at her photographs. The white Jerusalem houses with their fences of barbed wire and warning signs in the fields; the powerful, endlessly complex hills and recesses; the naked desert-like earth and pearl-gray edifices whose boundaries were as open to interpretation and vulnerable to disintegration as lines drawn into the dust.

My mother put the photographs back in the envelope and slid them into her dress pocket but, when she shifted in her seat, they spilled to the floor. The reading light passed through her uncombed hair. "My sister Esther inherited the house on Metaduleh Street," she started to explain. "Did I ever tell you how it was in Israel? Now Esther is married to Yakov Hendel, who lives in my father's house with her. And your grandmother. I think Yakov is only in the ministry of hostels, a low position and he doesn't have much money of his own. What a shame for Esther when all our friends married diplomats or generals after the war and built their own houses."

"I think you told me all this already," I said.

"You look like him."

"What?"

"Like my brother, Elizar. When you were born, I swore it was Elizar come back to me."

I looked down at the floor, trying to see whether any other photographs had spilled there.

"Get some sleep," my mother said. "We will be there before you know it. You must learn to be a survivor, Liana. Do you want me to take your hand in mine? Will it calm you?"

Two summers ago, my mother lay on the bed in Katonah, rolled up in the white sheets and pillow, and stuffing handfuls of them into her mouth, biting them in a rage of grief as my father sat at the desk table where he worked in the bedroom, reading the newspaper. There had been a fight. It was about money, and how the car he had bought was "theatrical" and "weak" like him, the blue MG which had stirred her into a tirade. It was not like other fathers' cars at the train station, she said. I heard them from the hall.

"Can't you do anything to quiet your mother?" asked my father when I walked into the room. He folded the newspaper page and read the next column. He wore tortoise-shelled half-glasses and smelled of Balkan Sobraine pipe tobacco." She wants you."

"I can't cope with your father when he gets like this," said my mother. She looked at him the way she would at a long-suffering child.

He said," I can't stand it either. I'm sorry." He put down the newspaper and went out the door.

I went to my mother.

She unhooked her bra, and her breasts fell out. "Stroke me. Do that, Liana," she said. Her hair was like a mashed apricot, still wet from the shower and the curls were dripping. "I told you to touch me," she said.

I put my hand on the small of her back, on the sweaty, dangerous flesh.

"Lower," she said. The sheets dropped from her hand, and her underwear was large and oily. She pointed to a spot above the rim of her panties. Calgon Bouquet bath powder and slick bath oil shone on her ribs. A thin but sugary sensation passed through me. I recognized it as love's involuntary and indiscriminate reflex. But disgust and humiliation, too.

I heard my father go down the stairs, and I stroked her. I breathed in the hot leak of my mother's pain. I did not get up to see where my father was going. I was a traitor to him, lost in the heat of the night. I lay beside my mother, putting my head down on the pillow where there were still some strands of his hair. The front door downstairs slammed. My father went to the garage, and I heard his car in the gravel driveway, the road out.

I picked up the pillow the stewardess had given me at the beginning of the flight and put it on my lap. The air was stuffy; it seemed dirty.

My mother was blinking her wide brown eyes at me. "I'm having a bad time in my sleep again, you know," she said. "Not because we are finally out of Katonah, but because when I close my eyes, I dream of what happened that made us leave our house in the first place. Now, leave it. Stop this whole discussion." Often, my mother talked as if someone else were in the conversation she was having with herself. She beat at the pillow strapped onto her seat. "I have to sleep. I have to be strong and think clearly when we get to Israel. Oh, you and your father talk so high on your kite," she slipped her tongue over one of the expressions she had picked up in Katonah, only it was from my father this time, not a television show.

I looked for the stewardess who had given us the pillows and my only Coke. She had vanished for good behind the curtains by the lavatories. Beyond us, deep white cigarette clouds billowed from the mouths of the other passengers unable to sleep, smoke puddled above the empty aisle.

The cabin light made a mirror out of the plane window. I stared back into a face that still looked like some brownie scout, the bobbed and nut-colored haircut, too round eyes. I had left the bulk of my belongings in a bag over our heads on our luggage rack, but I had my small purse, filled with the overwrought make-up designed to put on my face like the evil eye. Rough and powdery brush foundation, mascara, and the eyebrow pencil that cut black lines under my eyelids. I could be off with everything I owned in a matter of minutes if the chance arose. Among my skirts and sneakers were all my folders filled with poems and scraps from books, like the things I imagined the people in my father's books kept, the people who fled to snow-covered mountains in Europe, to recover from tuberculosis and other illness. I can't say I was certain that the best way I would rejoin him would be by taking own my life, but the notion of suicide hooked into my imagination. It seemed like a gracious thing to do, if you didn't lose your nerve. The thought stayed over, and, now and again, came to call. The idea that there were cathedrals and pleasure houses in Paris where sitting under pristine stained glass I could touch my father again became very real to me as time went on, or that I could jump back into the undefined dreamy splendor of my father's promised land, back into the way things used to be.

"Are you better now?" My mother asked me.

"What?"

My mother put her hand over my left fingers on the seat. Then she let go and picked a blanket up off the plane's floor, took it out of its cellophane, and threw it out.

"It's going to be all right, Liana." The blanket went up and spread in the air like a sail, falling and covering us. The silky material of my mother's tent dress flowed out even under the blanket, touching me. And then, there was a peace I felt, and everything was soft and dark and tingling.

I looked towards the floor of the airplane, her bare toes looked larger than they really were in the darkness and almost alive, like fleshy, shelled animals or fish. I reached up and turned off the reading light above our heads.

My mother's arms flopped carelessly at the sides of her body. Her head soon came to lie on the edge of my left shoulder. Under me, the plane engine began to sound as though it was growling.

I fidgeted with the threads in my bluejean skirt. I jostled my mother's head. My mother sighed and shoved her pillow to the high left corner of her seat. She laid her head there, her back to me.

Out the window, the space under me was turning to charcoal cumuli; dark, fluffy bumps that, in the moonlight, looked like a flock of black sheep. Only a dissemination of things could be found, detected in a vastness. Everything that was once solid form under me had sunk somewhere else.

The whole cabin was floating with the silent heave of my stomach muscles hoping to expunge my mother's closeness. I sat up as erect as I could on the plastic plane seat. Even that move jammed my thoughts together, shook up all the information I constantly arranged in my head. If I drifted off my mother would get through my skin and plant her alternate world of chaos and abandon inside me—the sudden warmth of her that smelled like salts, and a rich and almond oil. I would not be able to help myself.

She cupped her hands under one side of her face and fell asleep. I tried to keep fully awake, but soon images came with an invitation to rest in this half dream-state. My mother caressed me in the half-dream, she pulled me into her and protected me. I surrendered, partaking of her love and then in the mental movements that were darkness and fragment I was making love to myself, seeing and touching myself from the dreamer's place of seeing, my body had doubled and contained the shift, the ending of which drew out breath like blood.

By seven p.m. New York time, the plane landed for its hour of refueling inside the gusty night of a mountain range, but its passenger cabin, and it's fill of sleeping travelers were quiet as a bevy of bones. The lights in the cabin were off, and all I could see outside my window was the gleam of Swiss airline fuel tanks and scaffolds.

My mother's eyes did not open, and the plane ascended into the black air again.

I watched the swelling morning clouds over the continent, a dawn was coming carrying a light storm, heaving winds. We would be in Israel soon, I told myself, and there would be time for escape and remedy.

A few hours later, the airplane was jolted by turbulence in the air. My mother sat up, startled. "Oh . . . what? What?" She said, blinking. She kicked at her red-tanned purse that had toppled out of the seat's pocket with the magazines and tissues she had tucked inside it.

"Nothing, Mom," I said, "you're all right. It's nothing at all."

She stared at me. And then, she fell back into her sleep.

I sat, wide awake for a while longer, watching the airplane's escape hatch where other warning signs were pasted in white-and-black letters, instructions on how to bolt out in time and land on an inflatable float boat in the ocean, in case of sudden descent, or irreversible mechanical failure.

I stared out the plane window and into the great black hole in the galaxy where my father had fallen. The possibility of escape through death lived inside me as some odd and exciting adventure. I listened to my mother's heavy breathing blend with the noise of the airplane's motor under my feet, and I promised to the spaces unknown into which we were traveling, from one world to another, soon I would make a new life.

The plane landed outside Tel Aviv, inside the thick of a dry heat wave, the next day. The turbines shut off and it was abruptly noon, Israeli time, as if there had been no dawn, no morning anywhere. Out my window, I saw miscellaneous aircraft parts and scraps piled on dormant cargo carts.

"Are you awake, darling? We're here. Liana. We've arrived." My mother's chocolate bar was gone, and her wide, blinking eyes were alert, protective. "I'm going ahead of you," she said and unlatched our overhead baggage rack, pulling her black weekend suitcase down and the overnight bag. "Wait until the aisles clear and then carry this bag. I am the one who knows what to do, you will only get lost."

Lightheaded, I felt relief in hearing my mother direct my movements.

I watched her hustle ahead with her black suitcase in hand. She disappeared down some stairs, out into the sunlight onto the rough, unpaved runway below us. A metallic smell, like rusted gun shells, wafted up from the exit.

Then: "Stay together," Ivy said. She gathered up her satchel and the cartons of Chesterfields she had put under her seat, and pinched me on the arm.

Ivy and I disembarked down the steel stairway moments later, our hair sweaty but our underarms washed with the tiny Ivory soap bars in the plane's bathroom. Our watches were still set at 10:30 pm New York time. We had each put on thick pancake foundation and globby mascara. Our make-up soon streaked as perspiration ran down our cheeks. We didn't have sunglasses on to protect us against the scalding sun.

"Stay cool," Ivy said. Across her left shoulder lay the thick leather strap of her huge leather satchel. Her boyfriend had pinned a button on it that said: "PUFF THE MAGIC DRAGON IS A DRUG ADDICT," its aluminum glittering in the blazing light.

I held tightly onto the overnight bag and followed her, trying to keep one hand across my brow, to shield my eyes. A few hundred meters beyond the crude landing strip of Lydda airport the land looked as if it were made of bread, everything on it was tan and white, except for the military zones that appeared like rashes in the sands with their barbed wire and army posts. Israel was a distant mass of raw, sandy banks and white stony hills.

I sped up beside Ivy, hearing a roar that, first, I thought must be city traffic somewhere, but it was the Mediterranean coast, the encompassing shoreline of palm trees and hot, coarse sand. We were somewhere on the outer edge of a city by the sea, and I watched the other passengers moving in through a distant door to a flat, one-story limestone shelter. As far as I could see, squinting beyond my sister, there were no trees or awnings to shade the trek to the airport terminal.

Ivy looked over her loaded shoulder back at me. "I had no idea it would be this damn hot here," she said.

One Hasidic family from the plane was still visible under the clouds; their vodka bottles loaded onto a toy wagon one of their children had on the plane. They ambled towards the steel door of the building, behind which I hoped my mother would reappear.

Then suddenly Ivy grabbed my arm and pulled at me to keep walking. "For your own sake, don't look around," she said. "Just keep walking in a straight line. I think a jeep is following us."

"*Shalom, giveret!*" I heard. Male voices and coarse laughter crescendoed into the winds close to our backs: "*Hello, Americanit! Nichmad me'od! Nichmad!*"

The jeep stopped by Ivy and me for only a second, a scoop of fingernails and knuckles going under our skirts. The hands were so hot they could have been just baked in an oven. Not even the wind could blow my skirt back down. It stuck to the sweat on my thighs, my girl's underwear.

I jerked to my right and looked into the polished machine guns on the backs of the green-uniformed soldiers. I didn't know I had closed my eyes until I heard the jeep and men speed away, the Beatles' tinny sounds disappear into the sweep of sand and wind.

Ivy said: "hurry" and "fuck them" and I trudged forward into the hot wind, trying to decide if what had just happened was strange because it was so foreign, or because it was just strange. Twelve hours earlier, we had been walking on the grounds of our Katonah home, in the lush green woods.

"Don't you dare look back again." Ivy usually blamed me for everything, but coming to the plain limestone building, she kicked open the door with one foot and held it open for me.

Inside the terminal, the smell and feel of sweat was like a dense lather. Two Immigration officials in berets and badges were directing the scattered arriving passengers. "Please show passport! *Shama, givarot shama!*" They waved the confused faces to a worn counter.

Out of a steamy chaos, I watched an orange kerchief flare up. It took me a few seconds to realize it was in my mother's waving hand.

She was standing all the way across the room, next to a tall woman who must be my Aunt Esther. Esther held up a handkerchief, too, waving it just once. Then she took off her huge black rimmed sunglasses, looking at us as my mother jumped around and flagged her kerchief.

My aunt was an ample, mannish woman resembling my mother, but more severe. She studied us with her hard, coffee-colored eyes, her red lipsticked mouth an anomaly in the rugged surroundings, an old luxury she had splashed on for the benefit of guests.

My mother came marching towards us. "Girls, there you both are," she yelled. "You don't have to go through customs." She was waving at the officer, holding up three passports, fanning them.

The officer's expression softened, and my mother said: "*Todah, todah,*" in a Hebrew I didn't understand. "I have it all arranged. Now come on. Your aunt has ordered a sherut for us. The baggage is coming down the chute over there." Incoming suitcases were tumbling onto the conveyer belt against the east wall of the terminal. "You girls get it. I'm going back to Esther. I don't want her to think anything is wrong."

I walked with Ivy, wondering when my mother had taken my passport and Ivy's, where the return tickets were, or had she took them, too, out of our suitcases? I would open all the suitcases and look as soon as we got to Jerusalem. I would dig my return ticket up, find out if I could cash it in for a one-way ticket to Paris.

While we waited for our bags, I watched other passengers who were held under scrutiny at a customs table containing all that remained of the lives they had left behind. Their faces contorted as they scanned the dirty, crude shelter with its scarred walls, the soldier's black boots, the stands of frying sesame balls dripping an oily brown mess on the limestone. Outside, the black taxis looked like dirty hearses in the bright sun.

"It's so bad," Ivy said, her long hair already sweat-soaked. "They're a bunch of turds."

My mother and my aunt, gesturing wildly to each other, both talking at once, both laughing, were totally unaware of our presence.

A line of departing passengers pushed past the two of them, going in the opposite direction, making their way back home to the airplanes on the runway we had just come from. Sunburned people dressed in khaki Israeli short-shorts, leather buckle sandals, and drip-dry shirts they would soon remove to get back into their American clothing. Just then one of our brown suitcases shot out of the chute in the ceiling. I lugged it off the belt. Ivy began to drag her suitcase across the rough stone floor.

A string of Israeli flags fluttered over my head from the ceiling. In the distance, my mother was kissing and hugging a group of coarsely dressed women and men. The group stood in front of a yellow sign in English and Hebrew: "REUNION."

I felt an elbow grind into my side. Suddenly, an officer was tapping me on the shoulder.

"You have seen this boy?" He thrusted a large photograph under my eyes. The boy in the photograph could have been in a high school back in Katonah with me. But older, a few grades higher up. He had a pleasant face, slight eyes, and a fresh crew cut. "You know him, yes?"

"I just got here." I shook my head.

"*Ma kah rah! Ma yesh! Ma yesh!*" My aunt muscled her way through the crowded terminal, shouting, "*Yaldah shel-lee!*" She pushed herself between the policeman and me with the flat of her hand. "*He lo mevinah. Lo mevinah!*"

I tried to understand the strange-sounding Hebrew, the gurgle of shouts.

"*Aaz kloom!*" He said, one of his hands jerking up into the air as he swerved away with his photograph.

My aunt took in a scraping breath and tightened her belt. Her straw hat was fastened to her head with big metal clasps; the linen straps of her bra fell from the shoulder holes of the sun dress she wore. I let her embrace me, squeeze my much-smaller body. "You must call me Doda," she said." Doda means aunt in Hebrew." Her breath on my neck smelled like roasted sunflower seeds and sesame oil.

"Yes, hello," I said.

"This is a very bad situation with a missing American," she said. "A diplomat's son. Let us not mention anything about the photograph and the policeman, all right, darling? You must take care of your mother, yes?"

I glanced into the distance. My mother's group was dispersing, an airport official removing the yellow sign.

"Terrible," Doda Esther said. "But you know we will not talk of our brother Elizar either. Your mother has told you, yes *mawtek*? Any discussion of Elizar is not to be. We will however go to the ceremony at the President's house for the heroes."

I dragged the valise as Doda Esther showed me all the way outside, to the parking lot.

"Esther!" My mother shouted from the opened door of a large, black taxi, her voice turned aggressive and tough just in the time that had passed since we arrived.

My sister was collapsed against the fender, smoking one of her Chesterfields.

"*Ma kah rah?*" My mother rasped with the strength drawn in from the old air of her childhood.

"*Kloom, kloom,*" Doda Esther said. She helped the driver hoist and fasten all our baggage on the top of his cab, spitting out small bursts of the incomprehensibly guttural Hebrew.

She and my mother slid into the front seat with the driver. Ivy and I climbed into the back. We pulled the three bucket seats in the center of the floor, mounted our legs on them. The taxi pulled out of the airport lot, and Ivy cleaned off a spot on her passenger window with her palm.

Soon, the sand dunes on the edges of Rehovot appeared outside with the gray waves of the Mediterranean. I watched my mother's profile against the naked hills. She put on an old straw hat my aunt had brought out from her oversized purse to protect her. Doda Esther was cranking down the window on the taxi door. Then she leaned over the front seat and tested our door locks and door handles. She rolled down Ivy's and my window too.

Outside on the shoulders of the raw tar highway, I saw lines and lines of young hitchhiking soldiers. They stood under the scanty shade of the pine and cypress trees with their thumbs out, heavy machine guns slung across their backs.

"I remember everything now," my mother said.

In a few minutes, the taxi stopped in front of the sandbags of a roadblock. A young guard, distracted by the heat, and wind, walked up to the side of the front passenger seat where my aunt had begun fanning herself with her bare hand. He knocked absentmindedly on my aunt's cheek with his knuckle, tapping at it.

"*Ma zeh? Ma zeh?*" Doda Esther's cry was enraged beyond what I would have expected.

"*Giveret . . .*" The boy tried to calm her, leaning into the window slot.

"*Lo yafeh, yeled!*" My aunt shouted and batted away his hands. I felt the dusty air at my nerves, as if it had crawled through my skin.

Meanwhile, my mother opened her purse to show more officials advancing on our taxi our passports.

An officer handed my mother's papers back to her and bowed to Doda Esther. "Sorry, sorry," he said. He spat out something ungraspable to the embarrassed young soldier, and then the taxi driver put his large black shoe on the gas pedal and we passed through our first military checkpoint.

For a long twenty minutes, the sherut followed a torturous, worn road that twisted and wound itself around endless limestone rifts and bald, sun-scalded hills. An erratic vista of newly paved tar roads and rough hills and moving convoys of loaded kibbutz trucks and army jeeps, honking at our sherut as they passed.

"*Yoffee, achshav.* Wonderful now. We have come upon them," my aunt said in English for our benefit. "You see the old Israeli tanks in the shrubs here, Ivy and Liana? We used these tanks in the War of Independence. We leave them in the bushes here to always remind us. They are shrines to us. I am not afraid of a few border incidents over water. Our family has been in Israel for four generations. And your mother and I, we had our role, too."

"Esther, really," my mother said. "The girls just got here. What do you want from them?" She laughed, it was not a ha-ha laugh, but a sad, little laugh.

"Okay, Ada-leh. Of course, I don't want the children to worry about this water problem," Doda Esther laughed. "But on the radio they will tell us soon if the talks with Jordan have made any progress."

"Good, good," my mother said. She was different already, giving an opinion in somber tones on a piece of news she didn't even know existed an hour ago on the airplane. Ivy and I exchanged eyefuls of what was meant to be our mutual resentment for having to be here. Then I put my face out the window, looking up. The sky was clear, unflecked, like a rolled out canopy of sunny lavender and rose. Off the narrow, dusty road 1940s army vehicles rusted in heaps under desiccated shrubs and pine branches. The air smelled like dried blood.

"These roadblocks are terrible," Doda Esther leaned into my mother's shoulder to explain," but never mind please." She suddenly remembered Ivy, and me. "We are glad that you are all here. We will not discuss politics."

The black plastic of the seat was hot against my thighs. Already, I understood there would be a list of things not to mention; that Elizar, the roadblocks, the photograph of the missing diplomat's son, the fight over water was part of some vast scheme and rules I would now have to learn.

"We can go into Masada on Sunday, by the sea," Doda Esther said. "There I know a family. Very nice. From Bethlehem. Near the monastery there. They are Muslim, of course. But, the older boy might go into our army." Esther tried to put her slipping bra straps back on her shoulders under her sleeveless sundress. "Masada is where I will bring them. They can be Israelis for one afternoon, it won't hurt them, Ada. I will tell them the stories the way I did for my own children, Yaron and Nurit. All the children love my stories. It is a crime your daughters know nothing about Masada. I will soon become hoarse from having to tell them all the stories because you won't, Ada."

My mother rolled her eyes, as if towards the clouds that were drifting in from the lavender-tinted peaks in the distance. "I will bring the girls from America to Jerusalem again," she said to Esther. "A few more times."

"They will forget," Doda Esther said. "I will bring them back next summer."

"It isn't enough, Ada."

Doda Esther made a sour face with her lips that were small and doused in cold cream.

"Never mind, Esther, I tell you," my mother said. "You are worse than the army."

"Your mother must be with her first family again to get over such an awful tragedy, don't you believe so?" Doda Esther turned around, to me. "I am so sorry about your father. For him to die in an accident like this . . ." Even though she was trying to be tender, the harsh Hebrew sounded as if she were pulling taffy out from the back of the throat. Then Doda Esther took her large sunglasses off her face and stared into our faces with her naked eyes. "She belongs here now. Do you not think so?"

"Let's not talk so much," my mother said.

"No, we never talk about things like this, "Doda Esther said. "We have been through a lot, haven't we, Ada?"

"Quite a lot."

"But now you are home again."

"Yes," my mother said. "On what day will they have 'The Ceremony of the Graves?'"

Doda Esther's hand touched my mother's shoulders, and I saw in her fingers that were thinner and more primed than my mother's own stubby ones, a protection offered, and that they had somehow reached back to my mother's childhood and their past. "You will see that the house has not changed a bit," she said to my mother. "And everyone, they still do everything the same as if the world outside Metaduleh Street were exactly as you left it. There will be a party at the King David. Your old friends you will see again there, I believe, Ada. Then a few days after this we will go to the President's House for the ceremony." She turned and looked at Ivy and me. " You will love the house, girls," she said. "You know your grandmother is called Savta in Hebrew. You must know some Hebrew words. We have our ways; you will see. But do not look so nervous. You are good-looking girls, I think."

My mother pushed one of her hands under the hat on her head, flattening down her sweaty curls. Then she cupped her fingers over Doda Esther's hand, still on her shoulder, and Ivy and I were barred from entering the delicate places of understanding and alliance between the two women.

"Of course, Ada," Esther said. "I have put the girl's upstairs in your old bedroom with you. I will explain to them about taking siesta in the afternoon. I will explain to them everything." Esther turned around again and looked at us. "Do you sing, Ivy and Liana? I don't know; the radio seems out of good songs. I am delighted you have come to stay in your mother's country at long last. Look on the sides of the road and see whether you find any rabbits. They are famous for turning up in the hills here. Watch for them, yes, girls?"

My mother did not take out her chocolate bar on the way to her old home. She passed us two of the "Wash and Dri" packets that she had taken from the lavatory in the airplane instead. Doda Esther fanned herself with her hand as the sherut drove through the endless hills and my sister watched the road for rabbits.

"Yes, here is where I once hiked with my friends," my mother said after a while. "I do not remember any rabbits. There are lizards as big as rabbits in these hills, though. Perhaps these are what you saw, Esther."

I put my arm out the window. I leaned into the hot wind as far as I could. I recited the names of all the bridges of Paris, but my mother's first life was flowing into me, momentarily illuminated and strange, like the land had an enchantment on it, No one said a word more.

As we got closer to Jerusalem, the sky became brighter, the light of the blazing sun had grown so strong, it gave the barren hills an ochre sheen that was flashing, incandescent. And when the sherut finally reached the end of the long route through and around the Judean mountainside, there was a burst of paved streets. Sudden clusters of newly erected, pearl-gray buildings. We had entered the city.

2

I RAN OUT OF MY GRANDMOTHER'S HOUSE onto Metadulah Street, rushing up the limestone walk.

"Hurry up!" My mother shouted from a bus stop up the street. I had been in Jerusalem a week.

"Where were you, Liana? I made the bus driver wait. Everyone is angry with you!" My mother said.

"Don't sit next to me, asshole," Ivy said, jumping up the steps ahead of me.

I followed her, dressed in coarse, khaki shorts. Doda Esther had ordered me to wear them if I went outside, onto the dangerous streets.

Israeli "grush" coins made a tinkling noise, swirling inside the change tank as the doors closed, and the bus took off towards Ben Yehuda Street, the new city's shopping district.

I inched myself down the rickety wood aisle, grasping onto metal hoops from the ceiling. The bus walls were pocked-marked with bullet holes and cigarette burns. The aisle was a rotting wood, like a prison galley's in biblical children's books.

University students and tourists took up the front seats. In the back, Arabic women in long dresses sat with their groceries; sacks full of jutting loaves of bread, tomatoes, oranges, and onions. The windows looked out on a monotonous stretch of pinkish-white limestone apartment houses and their courtyards.

My mother was already sitting in one of the worn wooden seats by a window, brushing off her sundress with a Kleenex, and pulling up her washed stockings.

Ivy had settled into a seat in the back. She liked to pretend in public places that she didn't know my mother and me. That she was a housewife, or a university student traveling alone. She was wearing her denim bluejean skirt and American gingham blouse.

"I hope you weren't upsetting your grandmother," my mother said to me. "I hope you didn't tell her Doda Esther, and I were fighting this morning. We weren't fighting anyway. This is just the way we talk."

"Mom—" I started.

"Pssst . . ." One of the Arabic women said, pointing to me.

"Liana, quiet! They are staring at you," my mother said.

The bus passed the tailor shop, and the pharmacy. I watched the decline of the sun out the bus windows. It was six-twenty p.m. I read the time from my mother's wristwatch.

I held onto the rim of the seat in front of me as the bus swerved, making its way around the paved hills.

"Now they are rebuilding everything," my mother said after a while, turning back to me. "I cannot pass here without becoming upset." She spit into her fingers and cleaned a spot on the dusty window. "We are not going to the shopping district on Ben Yehuda I have decided, Liana. Elizar is everywhere. Do you think he is trying to speak to me again after all these years?"

I tried not to look away from her.

"Do you think I'm crazy, Liana?" She asked.

The Arabic women, hearing my mother talk to me like this, laughed. They took out shelled and salted hard-boiled eggs, eating them from cloth napkins spread on their laps.

Ivy was staring out the window in the back, at the promise of the new city from the distance. Ivy's eyes, contemptuous and cold when they gazed at my mother, now grew peaceful, turned away from us, as if from some horrible swamp.

She was happier on the bus, pretending she was not with my mother and me. "Don't look back at me," she mouthed at me. Then she put her right hand over her lips.

I turned back to my mother.

"No, Mom, I don't think you're crazy," I answered my mother's question. But, my mother no longer remembered asking it, her eyes wide and distracted.

The rattling vehicle took us through an area where the dry dirt, shrubs, and wild fields on both sides of the road were partitioned and there were no military stations or high walls forming the jagged border between Jordan and Israel: metal wires had been hung, tacked up between tall posts like hosiery lines. There were places in the fields where large family houses were cut in two with the wires, one half in Israel and one half in Jordan. I studied the fragile borders of the turbulent, divided land.

"Liana, it has been many years since I saw this place." My mother looked uncomfortable, as if she'd rather get out, walk in the fields. She tugged at the sleeves of her light sweater, then ran her fingers through the damp nylon of her stockings. She shook out her legs and fluffed out her sundress—a bright orange with iridescent circles. I looked at my mother, who had no respect for boundaries. She was straining to understand the unfamiliar, recently erected modern buildings in the distance, the borderlines between the paved and pearl-like Jewish State and Jordan's scrambled outskirts.

The bus moved faster, coursing up a steep hill. Soon, I could hear the muffled chanting marking the closing of the day. The men I pictured from the Muslim shops and streets were bowing in a mosque behind a large limestone wall, as the tall minarets of gold and silver behind the Gates of the closed-off ancient city bounced into view. As the bus neared Mandelbaum Gate, the Arabic women in black chiffon tarhas with silver-threaded shawls around their shoulders formed a line at the door. I rubbed my nose at the salty sweat smells of their thick, embroidered habaras, their heavy black stockings.

The bus slowed down to let the Arabic women off at the entrance gate.

Suddenly, my mother got up from her seat, as if she saw someone waving to her from on top of the incomprehensible stones that were forbidden to us.

"Look," she said, nudging me. "See the Gate? It used to be that we could go into the old city, before the War of Independence. My father's store is in there, but they bombed it now."

"*Leshevet, beh-vaka-shah*, sit down please," the bus driver said, glaring at my mother from his rearview mirror.

"*Shama, zeh Beit Meshuggeem?* Over there, is that 'The House For The Crazy'?" My mother asked him, sweetly. Then she walked forward and tapped him on the shoulder.

"*Beh-vaka-shah*, please," she said, pointing to Mandelbaum Gate, and to a cluster of goats and beggars below us. "*Po.* Here. I go, too. With my daughter."

She looked back at Ivy as I stood up. My sister was brushing her long hair.

"Ivy, you go ahead, darling," my mother shouted to her. "Liana and I, we will get off here and meet you back at the house."

Looking up from the dried, desolate soil after going down the steps with my mother. I could see the back of my sister's head, her long hair inside the autobus as it took off again.

My mother pulled at my hand. "Now, only be still, Liana. Be quiet and walk with me," she said. "Talk to no one and then we will be safe. My dress is American, and your face, my Liana, is American enough for both of us. Liana. This way . . . ." We kept walking towards the guarded Mandelbaum Gate. Sucking in our bellies, making ourselves small, we stopped and stood on the dangerous strip of border.

"*Raga ahod*—Wait a minute. Wait." One Arab guard pulled a machine gun up his shoulder. His hand went out, in the queue between the last Arabic woman and my mother. "You. Wait," he said.

"May I help you?" My mother said to him. "Is this Israel I am in? But, I want to be in Jordan."

"*Americanit?*" He asked

"Of course," my mother said. She opened her purse and took out a tourist map and a tiny brownie camera she had bought for our trip to Masada next week.

Was it the brownie camera? My mother's smile? The American sundress? It was a full cycle of excitement that my mother and I lived in for ten or fifteen minutes as we held on to each other oblivious of any other passage of time that might forbid us our happiness. We got by the guards. Crossing onto a busy quarter on the other side of the border.

The blood rushed through my head. Buoyant with light and color, the market street throbbed, the swell of bursting activity and fruit-filled aromas mesmerizing. Outside tents and stalls, fabrics hung on clotheslines. Donkeys and goats were tied to stone posts. Inside the rows of stalls there were beautiful things: brooches, necklaces, and earrings made of tarnished silver; purple and black smock dresses; strips of satin and lamb's wool, and olive wood religious artifacts.

Could I describe it? Stone and semen, a smell of bowels and body that was sweet. Here was a place nothing mattered but the senses. I was swept into a numbing paradise of things, standing with my mother. I forgot what we had done to get there: the Arabic guard station, the bus ride. I forgot that we had left Ivy alone on a bus, and even that Doda Esther was waiting for us, preparing our Friday night meal.

"Yes, yes," my mother said, wanting to take a taste of the many sweet Arabic cakes and to buy some of the tarnished jewelry and bring it back home with us, or some of the embroidered cloths. What war? Her eyes seemed to ask. "Let us stand here and look," she said. "Quiet, though darling, all right?"

"Yes," I said.

We walked further into the center of the city, down the smooth stone ladders. My mother had my hand, and the air was scents: fried fish, figs, Turkish candy rolls, roasting seeds and lemon juice.

"*Tov*," my mother said. "Everything I will buy for you, Liana, like before. And what else will we have this evening, Madam?" She took out a Kleenex and began dabbing at her lips, trying to spread her lipstick on them because its color had faded.

There was a dignity to my mother I didn't see in the heavy hours at One Metadulah Street. She was young again and walking through the past, Wolf Silberfeld's daughter with the gifts in her room from all the different parts of Europe my grandfather had business affairs in, who inhaled the fragrance-saturated air and smiled with her big lips and teased.

She grabbed at the fingers and held my hand tightly. She pulled me along by her side, and we squeezed past four or five other Arabic guards, drinking water from their metal canteens in a dirty vestibule, a "suq" that continued winding around some limestone columns where the smell of rose water drifted on the air, and the smoke of roasting seeds around a bend.

Shelves and pantries inside old shops held glass storage jars full of colored spices and honey, eggplant slices in jars of thick olive oil and whole red peppers. I watched the cleansing of the Arabic houses in the distance, rugs beat outside painted wooden balconies by large women holding straw brooms that looked like rackets.

"I hear there is war?" My mother called to a turbaned merchant standing in front of a stall of hanging silks and satins. "How foolish for us. I used to get these when I was a little girl." The man nodded at my flirting mother. Her brown eyes coyly blinked. "Here, now, Liana. You will be all right," She said. "But of course you are uncomfortable here. We will find you a habara to wear. I am certain. Now you are good. Very well. But, gradually she took off again. I followed her close behind, pushing through wildflowers and cacti that sprouted between slabs of corroded cobblestones in an expanse of vacant courtyards.

"This section here is like before the war," my mother said. "Now it's deserted. I am not afraid to come into these sections. That house over there must have been built by architects from Amman. Your grandfather took in commissions for them. They were in business together."

I watched her fingers as she tossed the loose curls of her hair. It was calming. I was giving into her as she talked knowingly about the strange places we walked.

The stained stone walkway stretched under a vaulted ceiling and my mother, and I walked through on the cobblestone. Thin eucalyptus trees growing up through the walk broke up the sundown. Bits of light scattered in. The cobbled walkway took us through an ancient hall of columns, and when we came out, we had arrived at a group living quarters where there were ritual public bathhouses and tombs. Two small nuns in black bowed in front of some ruins, and a priest with a scarlet-red Russian turban was smoking a cigarette beside a church door. He saw us and crossed the vestibule.

"I am American. Christian. Does it matter?" My mother began, and he waved us along, away from him.

Turning another corner, we walked under an arch outside the church walls and I kept my head low and was quiet.

Some more Jordanian soldiers were chain-smoking by squalid piles of tossed garbage and metal scraps.

We quickened our pace, entering a walled quarter with wide arches of rosy stone and flat, single-story rooftops that looked older than the Roman columns. Men in white turbans, all staring at us, padded barefoot through the courtyard gardens full of marigolds and tamarind trees. We soon drifted into vaulted souks below the Ottoman towers, towards blaring taped Arabic music which sounded like a swarm of bees.

A crowd was at the next bazaar, and I came to move more confidently, next to my mother, believing my appearance not to be so foreign anymore. And it was fun. Had become, or was becoming fun. But, I didn't know exactly why, treading through the thick seductive air, I felt this way.

"You don't have to think so hard," my mother said to me. "We'll eat something soon. We'll drink ginger ale maybe."

Early evening had made the air cool. Kerosene lamps were burning by doorways. There were even a few electric lamps under the tents of vegetables and nuts. Where the moon rose over the limestone ruins, the borders, and boundaries were almost invisible.

Shoppers were gathered around wheelbarrows filled with crates of fruits and vegetables, exchanging lira, currency from the Israeli banks.

We walked past more Arabic guards, and my mother smiled at them with her big lips. The dense air was filled with the unrelieved perspiration of the men. Their army posts were made of rocks and sandbags. Far in the distant hills, crumbling Arabic houses blurred into a maze of sacred domes and mosques. I could still see the surrounding mounds and hills.

Then my mother took a wrong turn. We walked into a blind alley, impassible. There were glazed blue doorways tucked into corners, lining darker, denser passages. I smelled the latrines near the holy sites, toilet holes.

Slowly, we came into an open square. Trash had been left to blow into shreds by the evening breezes.

"It was good that you were quiet," my mother said. The refuse didn't bother her, or the squalid stone. "No, we won't be going down where there is no light again. Here there is more light."

I had not seen the band of boys approaching us, six of them, dark-skinned teenagers.

"Lira, please, missus! No speak!" One barefoot Arab boy ran up to me. He opened his left hand, flashing a box of brooches and some stones. "Look, missus, stones from the Holy Land," he said. My mother grabbed for my hand. "You must be extremely careful here, Liana," she said. "You must do exactly as I say, do you hear me?"

The stench of donkey urine fumed up the alleyway. I looked down and saw what the first Arab boy had been carrying in his other hand—a few plain stones that were wet and crumbly, like old hardened clay.

Then three other boys circled my mother and me.

"Very beautiful stones," the first boy said to me. "I sell to you only. Souvenir."

On the top of the Arab boy's shaved head there were scabs, flies were stuck to his street-dusted nose. The boy coughed. His lungs

sounded bad. Clumps of Nescafe powder had stained under his fingernails and hardened on his bad teeth. In the alley, their shredded sleeping cots and broken bicycles lay on the cobbled street.

Beyond us, further up on the Jordanian hills I saw tourist hotels with
water sprinklers and carefully gardened flower beds. "Buy, *yaldah*, girl,"
the first boy said to me. "Please, please."

"Stop!" My mother said. "We are not tourists. I was born here. I am
Sabra, *yeled*. Stop this!"

"These stones maybe from where you were born," the first boy said.

"Little miss," the boy said to me, coming closer. "Buy, buy." His
eyes seductively fastened on me, the same dark brown as the espresso
in the Arabic cafes. He showed me the ordinary stones in his hand.
"Ooo-ahh—" he said, as though he was offering me gold. "Souvenir,
missus. Please buy."

The other Arab boys stepped away now and waited for him to finish selling.

"How much is it?" I asked the boy.

My mother yanked at my hand. "Liana, *sheckit*. For God's sake,
Liana." She turned to the boy. "She doesn't know anything," she said
to him. "You are not to come near her, do you understand?"

"*Lama*? Why?" He asked. He pointed his dirty fingers at my khaki
shorts. "*Yaldah shel'ach*, AC/DC? Your girl is AC/DC?"

The other boys laughed, circling us again, their hands reaching for
my mother's pocketbook. "AC/DC," they shouted. "*Lo, yaldah!* Not a
girl! *Lo, yaldah!* Not a girl!"

"That's not nice," my mother said.

"I can have the daughter, missus, even if she's AC/DC. Look, look!"
The first boy shouted, and he started to unzip his shorts.

"Shoo!" My mother shouted to all the boys. "Yallah! Go! You will not
touch her! Do you hear me?" My mother lifted me up and began running
very fast down the alleyway. She ran through the stone carrying me under
her arm, my legs kicking and I felt the sphincters in my stomach loosen as
if I were going to heave out and then dissolve, but when she put me down
on the ground again, it felt hard and I was dizzy, standing on it.

"Liana . . ." My mother put out her hand to steady me. It felt like a tiny tree that was clasping onto me. "Don't fight me, Liana," she commanded. "You don't understand."

"What do you mean!" The pain in my ribs from her hold was subsiding, which brought me only the fact that we were in a hole full of moldering garbage and stone.

"One more minute, please." My mother wiped her finger across my face.

"In my eyes," I said to her, "the dust. Get it out."

She felt for my eyes with those fingers. Her left forefinger pushed itself into the moist whites, the unsuspecting ball and retina. When she withdrew it, I blinked, stung. She pressed up against my side. In the dark, her breathing was loud, and soft, and, in my confusion, I looked up at the early moon. I saw some lavender clouds through the crumbling turrets, a swell of moistures, and night. The air brought to me a sense of nausea, even disgust, and repulsion, then all shifted into a tingle, immersion, excitement, and thrill.

"You want some mineral water?" My mother asked me after a few moments.

She bent, kneeling down on the stone.

I put my foot flat. Still bent down, she adjusted my sandal buckles. When she stood up, she took hold of my elbow.

"I hate these shorts," I said. "Why did you and Esther make me wear these shorts?"

"Liana, what has gotten into you?" My mother's hand went up in the air, as if she were going to slap me, but she stopped and stared at me, her brown eyes widening.

"Stop treating me like I'm a baby," I said.

"Keep your voice down, Liana. You are a baby if you start up on a street like this. We are not where it is all right just to scream."

"These shorts make me look like a boy." I started pulling at the shorts' cuffs, as if I could break all their threads, and the two shorts' legs would turn into a skirt.

"But you liked them," my mother said, watching me." Didn't you want to wear them?"

"I'm not a boy."

My mother grabbed my hands and made me stand up straight. "Don't be silly," she said. "No one thinks you're a boy. These boys, they meant me perhaps. They think I am AC/DC."

"I know what it means," I said. "It means I'm abnormal. People think I am not a girl."

"You are mistaken." My mother brought me against her chest, kneeling down on the rough stone. "Do you know how much I love you, Liana? Do you know? Liana, how much? How much?"

The shorts felt heavier when she said that, and they made me sadder, but I didn't tell her.

"Here is where I lived when I was your age," she said, "I wore shorts like this. Do you think you will find it in your heart to walk with me now, my lovely girl, Liana, who no one could ever mistake for a boy? We can forget all that just happened."

I nodded.

She took my hand again. We walked further, into a labyrinth of old stone edifices, through the colonnades, and the bazaars where other merchants waited, squatting and lighting water pipes and hookahs. She said: "Stop." And we stood still to hear the chanting by a silver-domed Mosque.

"Oh, look, Liana." My mother pointed to a stand of candies and nuts. "All sorts of sweets, and Doda Esther isn't here to yell at me. You want?" She asked me. "It is safe."

She took me to a stocked stand shining with multicolored, rolled jellied treats, like a pastel glow of my mother's strange happiness as her eyes glanced through the busy Arab quarter. "How much are these sweets?" She asked the merchant. She let my hand go, and took out some lira from her purse.

The merchant gave her two bags of the candies, and she placed one of the bags in my hand. She lifted up four confections made in the shapes of tiny lemons and watermelons and motioned for me to find some to eat from my own bag. I took three confections out of my bag and stuffed them into my mouth, chewing. My belly filled with the tart treats which were heavily sprinkled with granules of table sugar.

"Your grandfather is buried up there, on that hill. That is Mount of Olives up there," she said, now pointing to a bushy hill that ascended in the distance. "I am never afraid of this quarter because I know my father is near me. Do you know how foolish this war is? That is why Savta is so strange these days. I think she is waiting for my father to come back from the dead and sell the new TVs from Tel Aviv to all our old customers in the Arab quarter here. This is how we used to make our living. We're near Dung Gate, near the Western Wall. It's called the Dung Gate because when the British were here they threw their garbage down from a bridge they built above our houses. When the bridge collapsed, the garbage was still there."

She took another Kleenex from her purse and patted her lips again.

"Let us go there," she said. "It is nearer to the hill."

Then we walked into an enclave of more debris and damp stone, and Dung Gate arched above our heads. We walked under it, into the refuse. I looked at the wristwatch on my mother's wrist. It was seventen. The sun and moon had exchanged places in the sky. I felt the dry dirt under my foot, sliding in over my sandals.

It was dark where we're walking and I was getting tired, my teeth beginning to hurt from chewing. I made myself stay quiet.

"Elizar and I did things we shouldn't have," my mother said after we walked a while longer But she was speaking with herself, not me, again. "Two children, you know. And always a war. We were so lonely. Doda Esther said if I had children they would be disturbed because of this."

"Because of what?" I tossed the nearly-empty bag of sweets into the other refuse and rubbed a finger under my teeth to scrape up the remains of the jellied candy.

"Nothing, Liana, nothing," my mother said. "We had this blanket in the basement, and we were always together when the bombings happened. We were very close, my brother and I. Children, they do things."

"Like what?" I tried to imagine my mother and her brother together under the blanket, playing British soldiers—my mother's younger, naked body full of enchantments. The emerging moon suddenly hurt, shining too soon and brightly, white arrows of light through the forbidden and dank tunnel we were walking through.

"Were you kissing?" I suddenly asked.

"No, nothing!" My mother cried, angry. "Don't ask me things." I bent to pick up some stones, our own souvenirs, and cupping the moist clay-like limestone in my hand I put some in my shorts pockets.

"I bring you to Israel, and you can see what a normal girl you are. And nothing is wrong with Ivy either."

"I want to go back to Metadulah Street now," I said. "It's getting too dark and I'm cold. I shouldn't have ever worn these shorts. It's freezing here."

"Look, Liana," she pointed to the foot of a small path on the hill. "Do you think there are spirits from the people who died? If so, we can find my brother. Here is the path up to the hill, you see? It is Fate that we find this path."

I glanced up at a bald zigzag of dry dirt which led to the top of Mount of Olives.

"I will climb this hill; I tell you and I want you to come with me. We will do it together. I will go first."

My mother hoisted her dress, determined. Her large eyes targeted the hilltop where we could only see some corroded boulders and pine trees sucked of their green. I watched her feet, she wiggled them, tossing her flats off. She took down her stockings, unlatched them from their garters, rolling them all the way down to her ankles and then, pulling them off, she dropped them in my hand. I held the balls in my palm.

"Do you think you can make it?" She asked me. "Put my stockings in your pocket."

Stuffing my mother's rolled up stockings in my short's pocket, I tracked up the barren path, crouched because if I walked straight I would lose my balance. My mother's freckled legs, her wide girth and back were in front of me, dry dirt kicked back. I shut my eyes so that the dirt wouldn't fly into them. I imagined the face of the lost brother, Elizar. When I opened them again, my mother was far ahead of me. I took long, leggy strides to the top of the hill where she waited for me in a quiet filled with moonlight.

"Oh, my God, Liana," my mother said and she kneeled where there was more garbage, but this time, gravestones, jutting up from the ground in messy rows, about fifty of them or more, friable and yellowed like human waste. There were some old gun shells lying here, too.

I watched my mother brush her skirt and clear her throat. Then: "Look at you," she said, taking my face in her hands. "You are not even a bit disturbed. Doda Esther should be ashamed."

Wrappers from the Turkish nut candies, foil, and scraps the soldiers had thrown for the stray cats crunched under our feet.

There were no shops here but epitaphs, it was a graveyard, this place, and I started to shake. I rubbed the sleeve of my shirt under my nose and coughed.

"Hush," my mother said." You have caught a cold, I think. But you must be quiet. Do you think I am kidding about the spirit from the dead people we have known? Maybe Elizar is here to see you now. I am glad I am not a Christian. They do not believe in the invisible world. You see if a soul was not happy, we say he lived on probation and he will come back in another body. Do you have a handkerchief, Liana? It's cold in this section. You are right. I am sneezing too."

My mother sneezed. There were more abandoned cats in the pine needles. My mother bent, and they went towards her, licking the fingers that had been into so many sweets and scents.

"Let's stay here and rest," my mother insisted.

I sat down next to her on a boulder, under a tiny beam of moonlight. The West Bank hills were only yards away. My mother's eyes turned towards them. "Jordan is there and the mountains. You cannot see from here. Now, I will tell you. It must be that the probation is over. My brother was sent away, far away somewhere, not here in Jerusalem. I try not remember. You will understand your mother, and not be so angry with her. I know you are struggling. You don't have to come out and say so."

I swallowed, but my mouth was dry. There wasn't any more candy inside it. I coughed to moisten my mouth.

In the moonlight, there was an edged beauty to my mother. The round woman looked glamorous against the barren debris, the garbage, and the graves, her bosoms asserted themselves into the stenchful air, amid the corrupted stone. Her presence was like a narcotic in this dirty place; the earth rose, aroused, swirls of dust that turned to intoxicating waves of wind and imagination. I envisioned her dancing in one of her silk dresses, her shoes off and her quick feet wild, a rough star of the underground with all her boyfriends. I could see my shadow when I looked into the stone, the throw of moonlight on the graves. I was so small against the large female person who was my mother sometimes and sometimes this character from the past, as sultry and sexy as any character I might read about in the British romance novels left in the closet at One Metadulah Street. Even in the ugly field of forgotten deaths here, she looked radiant and carnal—her rippling flesh, freckles and broad, full-lipped face. It was dizzying, death and decay and my mother's perfumed, sex smell.

"When Ivy was born I was still mourning for Elizar," she said. "It is why your sister doesn't like me. She wants no part of being Israeli."

The evening wind went through the underside of my sandals like a tongue, my legs were shorter than hers, I thought, and I put my hand under my shirt to feel my breasts. I put my hand to touch the tiny bumps that I hope will make me like her. I studied my mother against the moonlight and the sky which made this place, like all of Israel, horrible and stunning at the same time—the graves that were strips of brittle stone, and the desiccated, naked ground. Then suddenly I heard the taunt of Arab boys again inside my head, the awful sting: AC/DC . . . AC/DC.

"Liana, really," my mother asked me. "What is the matter with you?"

I couldn't again tell my mother what was bothering me. That I still thought I looked like a boy. I looked at all the stones, around at the hill.

She loped her finger across my cheeks. "What?" She asked me. "Don't put your hand in your shirt. This is a silly thing to do. What're you doing now with this hand of yours?"

"I had a problem, that's all," I said, putting both of my hands quickly inside my pocket again.

"What? What kind of problem?"

"An itch," I told her.

"I should not have told you all this about my brother. You are always too sensitive, Liana."

"It's cold here," I said.

We were silent. It was quiet and dark and peaceful, the air was cooler and the vines and desolation went all pearl-like under the moonlight, like phantasms.

I waited, seated with my mother on the rock.

"Okay, enough then!" She said after a while, slapping both of her palms against her thighs. "You should have taken one of the sweaters Doda Esther lay out for you before we left. Come, let's get off this rock. He will be back, Elizar. This probation has lasted long enough, I believe."

My mother was the first to go down the hill, her legs bare and soiled. Her hand reached behind her back for mine, but then she saw she could make it down the path without me, and she followed the dry dirt, her strong shoulders falling further from my view as I went behind her.

She waited for me at the end, standing on the flat ground, her hands on her hips.

"I am glad that we went all the way up. I will remember it when we are back in Westchester, and I think again about my brother and my father," she said. "Give me my stockings now, Liana, so that Doda Esther cannot accuse me of not being a lady when we get back. Oy, I am getting too old for these adventures, I think. But, you know Liana; it is good to be a woman! I remember now. It is good."

She lifted up one foot at a time, cleaning off her toes with her handkerchief, and then she put a hand on my shoulder, balancing herself and pulled each stocking up, over her foot and inside the latches of her garters again.

A swelling crowd of Arabic shoppers and some foreign tourists with straw hats on their heads appeared in the distance. My mother and I began walking again. Then the street we came upon was busy with colors, the fresh, cool evening.

"You see, we have come to another Muslim section," my mother said. "*Yallah*. Forget the past now. Keep walking with me. You must trust me, Liana."

We turned a corner, and around us the blue cement houses and small mosques carried the dank sweaty odor of sleeping bodies, but the stone smelled sweet; yesterday's rainwater had been captured in the funnels, golden ducts, and puddles wet the dry scabby feet and parched faces, kneeling and praying now, turned to the East, the vast strangeness of nightfall.

My mother took out some lipstick and put a streak on my lips and rubbed it for color." Come quick, though," she said.

I felt the prickly evening coolness on my bare calves, tasting the make-up.

"I will show you, Liana, what a girl you are. You see up just a little way in the Armenian quarter is a store that says: Linens. I remember it from the old days. It is in English, this sign, do you see it? It is only for girls and for women. As soon as you enter this store, it will tell you, of course, you are a girl, and to stop your silliness. I have decided we will not wait to buy you a dress. Why wait for tomorrow? Quickly though. We must get back to Metaduleh Street before Doda Esther suspects where we have been."

We hurried through another alleyway. The Armenians were gathering to get their fruits and vegetables for their evening meals, exchanging modern currency from the Israeli banks they were allowed to do business in during the day for older Arabic silver coins and bills as change.

Outside the dress shop, the merchant had already seen us and was holding up a long, black Arabic dress.

"Here, missus," he shouted at us. "Special for you. All the people want this dress only."

My mother halted, let go of my fingers, and took the dress from the man's hand.

"Come, come," she said to me, and she held the dress under my chin, spreading out its silky black skirt over my bare legs and shorts.

"You want it?" She asked me." It's yours. And no more that I treat you only like a baby and that you look like a boy. That I have to listen to you saying these things gives me a headache. I can't tell you anything. You are more sensitive than is normal. I get you this dress, and you wear it."

Inside the store, there were shelves of folded linens and hanging baskets filled with balls of yarn and buttons. The merchant poured himself some espresso from a silver pitcher on his counter. He sipped from a tiny cup, watching my mother take me to the mirror. My mother's feet looked small on the pearly stone.

The dress was long like the Arabic women's on the bus. Its crisscrossing embroidery threads hand-sewn in bright gold and blue and white.

"You have something my daughter can put on when she takes off all her clothes? A towel maybe?" My mother asked the merchant. "I want her to try on the dress. You will have to take off these ridiculous army shorts, Liana. I will hold a towel around you if he gives it to me." "Please—Liana we are not in Bloomingdale's."

"You have also a store?" The man asked my mother, putting down his cup. "Where is this, Bloomingdale's?"

"No, no," my mother moaned.

"You have many friends who perhaps have stores in America?" He asked her.

"Many friends," she said. "Good connections. Maybe you can meet them if you come to my home in America. How much for this dress? How much do you want?"

"Over there," he pointed to a folding screen in the back of the store. "Undress there. I don't look. No one will see. We will talk business."

"Liana, go," my mother said.

I took the dress and walked to the back of the store, slipping behind the folded screen. My mother handed me a towel and told me to put it around my waist and then to take off my shorts under it.

I felt the tender linen as the gown went over my head and then fell on my shoulders, and I pulled it down, down to my calves and ankles. I could hear the merchant and my mother talking from behind the screen.

"Why you come behind the wall now, Missus?" He asked my mother.

"I don't understand these things," my mother pretended, flirting, her voice soft and girlish.

Wrapping the towel around my waist, I slid down my shorts. I could see the back of my mother's coiffure as I craned my neck around the folded screen to look at them.

"Do you know that now the guards will make us have a curfew, before sundown on Fridays?" My mother was asking the merchant.

"Terrible. Everything very bad," he answered.

I looked in the mirror that was smudged and smelled of sweat and old yarn. My nose looked longer; there was a thickness to my thighs. They had rounded and felt different. The dress was inky black with a design of threaded doves on its chest, and it flowed out covering me, my flat chest and bony neck.

I heard my mother flirting again with the merchant. This is how my mother bargains, I thought. I wonder whether the man is coming back on the plane with us to America, and if he will be in my house . . .

"Liana!" My mother shouted back at me after a while. "What is taking you so long? I am here for my health? Hurry up already."

I started to lift the dress up from the hem, bending, but then I stopped, stood straight and let the dress cover me again, running down my hips and legs, liquidy—a pouring of night-black cloth. It drowned me in a change I didn't have words for yet. I died, but I came back, a casualty of some other world. The dress pulled me up, into the new world. I was not a boy, or no one at all. I saw myself in the mirror standing beautiful as the young Arabic women with their children and hand-baskets of fruits. "Liana, hurry or we will miss supper," I heard my mother in front of the screen and the black dress was cool and lightweight. I dropped the old army shorts I had been holding in one hand.

I stepped out from behind the screen.

"Wonderful! Look! Look!" The merchant cried.

It seemed that all my life I was attached to my mother, like a shadow to a ray of light. But now she backed away.

"Liana, it is like a dream for you. You are beautiful now," she said.

"Come in the back room, I show you more dresses, Madam," the merchant gestured to my mother. "How young is this girl you have?"

"No, no," my mother protested. "It's my daughter I have told you, and we do not go into any back room; I assure you."

"As you like," the merchant said." But she is, indeed, beautiful."

"I pay you forty lira, not fifty. I'm American. I only carry so much lira."

"No, no," the merchant said. "Forty-five. I tell you—you cannot always find a man to tell you your daughter is beautiful. Forty-five lira, Madam."

"I pay you forty-two. Remember I have connections."

"Aach," the merchant groaned. "Then forty-two. But, perhaps you would also like some linens. Also, a good price because you are a beautiful woman like your daughter."

"What would I do with linens?" My mother said. "I could tell you a few things about linens, you know."

"Madam," the merchant went back behind the counter and brought out a plain paper bag for me. He put my shorts and my shirt in it, "Take. Forty-two. As you like, Madam."

"Liana, wear this dress," my mother said to me. "And you will see. These boys, they really wanted to kiss you, maybe this is what made them so cruel."

It was even darker on the streets when we left the store. The alley-ways were almost empty of tents and merchants, only soldiers were out by the buildings, smoking.

My mother stood back and examined me in the light of the growing moon. "Look at this dress you have!" She shouted. "Did you see how we did it? This was fun, wasn't it, Liana? Now we go back to that awful house with my sister. We will tell her we got the dress in the new city. Just promise me you will say this. It is not for her to know about our little adventure. Promise me."

"I promise," I told her.

We walked until we saw Mandelbaum Gate again. The sentries were still there, but my mother pulled at me, and I went with her to a place where old stones had collapsed, creating a large opening in the wall.

Beyond it, some corroded barbed wire had fallen, no longer strewn across the area on the other side and, exposed, we could see the square we had first arrived in, where the bus had let us off. "You go through, first," my mother said to me.

I wished I could take the dress off, but the soldiers by their posts were too near. I lifted the dress up to my shins. My knuckles scraped against the sharp stones as my mother pushed me.

"Liana, hurry," she whispered. "The bus will be the last by here this night. I think the merchant knew that we were Jews. It was dangerous now. We must hurry."

My mother pushed herself through after me.

I stood up straight on the other side of the wall. The dress tumbled all the way down to my feet again. It had ripped when I kneeled on the barbed wire but in the dark my mother couldn't see the tear. And I brushed it with the back of my hand.

"Beautiful girl," my mother embraced me. "Like Sophia Loren. Pretend you are Sophia Loren." White dust had drifted into her orangey hair, and she shook her head. She scratched it, her coiffure, laughing. For these seconds, I was fulfilled, nothing could hurt me, or the person I was with, I am swollen with love, I thought.

I held my head up the way I saw the Arab women walk, and my mother took my hand. Then she walked ahead of me, taking out her last stack of grush for the bus ride back to Metaduleh Street. From the back of her head, she could be one of the guards or a man, I thought—the stout, fiery body and the way she marches. I did not let myself think more about this. My mother took out her Kleenexes and wiped us down as we waited for the autobus to come and take us back to Metadulah Street.

The Friday night meal began punctually at eight o'clock that same evening.

I came into the dining room on time and pulled out my chair. I had hung the Arabic dress in the bedroom closet and promised my mother I would say nothing about our trip into the old city.

My sister was blowing at her newly-polished fingernails. She wasn't talking either. She was watching the Biblical pewter, and glass implements on the table catch whatever accidental moonlight came in from the curtainless window. Were the faces and instruments finally intimidating her?

Zorah, my grandmother's Turkish friend, was here, on the right hand side of my grandmother, Savta, seated at the head of the table.

Zorah had a strong, beak-like nose. She was a Druid and much younger than my grandmother though she also had long, gray hair. Her eyes were almost silver, and her long legs graceful. She wore leather pumps in the style of the working women in the new city but, now retired from teaching high school and widowed, wrote children's books and liked to tell stories. Two days ago, when she came to play cards with Savta, she told Ivy and me a story about how the world was dark and full of war before Israel was born, and a story about other Arab Druse who had escaped the British jails in Rehavia and then joined the resistance for the Jews in 1947. That same afternoon, I heard Zorah tell three other stories, but about the British Tommies catching nasty flus and allergies when they searched for escaped Haganah men who, unlike our conquerors and European colonizers, could withstand the barren surroundings and its remains. Shuffling a stack of playing cards yellow with age, Zorah had continued with a story about a famous British captain suffering a "nervous breakdown"; he was shipped back to London in a straitjacket because a few Haganah boys put a donkey in his bed while he was sleeping, she had said. My mother and her brother were so wild they bathed in the nude by the sea, Zorah added. And, in the fields and orchards, when the rainwater fell, my mother and Elizar ran naked through the puddles of Quiriat Anavim, amid drenched oranges and chicken feathers. The grown-ups of Metadulah Street could always tell when my mother had been out past her curfew, Zorah finished, because my mother could not wash the smell of oranges and chicken feathers off her skin for days.

I watched Savta as she tried to see whether there was food already placed on her plate, squinting her bad, almost blind eyes and running her chaffed forefinger across the china plate.

Sitting in my chair on Savta's left side, next to my mother, I smelled my grandmother's fragile body. She gave off a scent like boiled milk and her wrinkled, white skin was like a fine, creased silk. Savta's face was still swarthy and childlike—her small nose and small mouth and high-set cheeks. She wore her silvery hair in a bundle wound as if it were yarn on a loom, and her hair was held in its fullness by gold hairpins with the symbols of the animals on their strips—Cabbala signs, and suns and moons.

"Liana," my mother poked me with her soup spoon. "Pass me a matzo cracker, will you darling?"

When the front door opened it was my uncle, Dod Yakov—Doda Esther's husband. I heard his wooden leg clacking on the stone floor of the foyer, and his coughing. The old clock on the trolley read: 8:05.

"I'm sorry to be so late!" Yakov said, lumbering into the dining room. " Shalom Liana. Shalom Ivy." He squeezed me on both shoulders, let go, and tossed his straw hat at the armchair in the back of the room. Parts of his fair skin were pockmarked, his nose was thick, his body bearish. His straw hat left rings around his closely-shaven head, indentations that vanished, red and raw at first.

Dod Yakov reached around my head and pinched my cheek. "What is for supper tonight, Esther?" He asked my aunt." I want that our guests should be satisfied."

Yesterday, my aunt had told Ivy and me that during the 1948 war Dod Yakov went to bring some bottles of milk in for the morning coffee. A little boy was in the bushes, playing near a live grenade. My uncle had rushed to save the boy, grabbing him up and running with him into the kitchen. The little boy was saved but Dod Yakov went back to get the milk. His leg caught the tail end of the grenade's explosion. When he walked around the house now, his bad leg pushed through his trousers, erect. It had to be amputated, his damaged leg. His good leg tried to keep pace with the thrust he had learned which made his hips muscular and wide.

Now his wooden leg scraped and knocked down on the dining room's hard marble floor. The shoe at the end of Dod Yakov's wooden leg was smaller than his other shoe, where his foot, and leg were still good.

"Dod Yakov makes quite an entrance, doesn't he?" Doda Esther said to my mother.

Dod Yakov ambled over to his chair at the opposite head of the table from Savta, and sat down carefully, his wooden leg bending on its false metal knee. His white yarmulke and an old prayer book had been taken out of the glass cabinet in the dining room and put on the tablecloth near his plate in front of him. Dutifully, he put on his yarmulke.

In the center of the table, the challah bread was wrapped in linens. It rested on a pewter platter engraved with mystical symbols on it: grapes and olive trees and the signs for health. Laid near the platter, a dish of baked chicken steamed from a glass serving dish.

My mother put a finger over her lips to tell my sister to be quiet. Then she indicated my grandmother, who was staring into the dish of chicken, squinting behind her bifocals.

"Let us begin!" Doda Esther clapped her hands in the air. Dod Yakov picked up a large, porcelain server of soup, scooped some of the liquid out and into my soup bowl.

I felt warm when I sat next to my uncle. His shirts were see-through, and I noticed his barrel chest and thought that before he lost his leg he was a handsome and strapping man.

"Try the potato soup," my uncle said. "You think it is so rough and hard, but it is also so good for you."

"What will be the theme for the stories tonight?" Doda Esther asked.

I looked around the room, nervous. The old articles from the old city, bought long before the borders, were rubbed, cleaned, and dusted daily; placed in a chestnut wood display cabinet against the wall.

My mother glanced at me sharply, afraid I would tell Doda Esther about going behind the wall earlier this night. But, I looked back at her, shrugged, and took up a spoonful of soup. My mother's face relaxed.

"Yes, Liana, eat your soup now," my mother said. "Esther will be telling us the same stories she does three times a day. This is the theme. I have just decided."

Portraits of my grandfather and my other two uncles, the ones who were not Elizar, were up on the walls—the departed Masters of One Metadulah Street.

The painting of my grandfather, Wolf Silberfeld, hung above our heads. It was mounted years ago, over a bullet hole one of British Tommies blasted into the wall when he came to search my grandfather's house in the midst of a seizure on the city. The brothers in the other paintings on the wall were named Yoram and Nathan. Yoram went to an American university in Lebanon and studied business. He moved away from Metadulah Street after the war, but he stayed in Israel. Nathan married an Austrian woman whom Esther had said was "too beautiful" and "did nothing with her life" but "go for pedicures and yogurt fasts" in the Haifa that had become "too large" and filled with boats from "too many" places. Yoram's dark-eyed wife was the daughter of a "bohemian" from Tel Aviv and their son, Esther had said, "already goes to discos with women who wear bikinis."

I studied the face of my grandfather, a broad-faced man with severe but light-colored eyes, wearing a fashionable European business suit. His thick hands were like Dod Yakov's; he was freckled, with bronze hair.

"Very nice painting, Yes?" Dod Yakov said, winking at me.

Then Doda Esther tapped her soup spoon against the rim of the table.

"Yakov, use a handkerchief," she said. "I see you are sweating. You are like a waterfall this night, Yakov."

My uncle picked up his cloth napkin and wiped his brow. His yarmulke suddenly slipped into the soup. He quietly picked the yarmulke out of the potato soup and asked: "May have a napkin please to dry it in, Esther?"

Everyone breathed out their laughter, like a unison of winds.

"Yakov, finish your soup," Doda Esther said. "Really, Yakov."

"You know Savta will lay her make-up out in the bowl in the foyer tonight, Liana," Zorah said. "She thinks your grandfather will be coming back on this Sabbath Eve. She told me tonight as I walked in the door. She was a beautiful woman once, your Savta."

I looked anxiously around at my grandmother.

"Do not worry. She cannot understand enough English to know I have told you her secret."

"Liana, you are not to go into Savta's make-up if you see it, do you hear me?" My mother asserted. "I heard you this morning in her room."

"Someday I fully expect to see another baby in your grandmother's belly," Zorah continued. "She is, after all, a lovely woman even now." Zorah scooped up some soup with her spoon, bringing it to her mouth and sucking the warm liquid through her lips.

Standing, Esther picked up her soup bowl and then fussed around the table, collecting all our soup bowls. She ushered herself, and the soup bowls into the kitchen, saying nothing more.

With a long face, Ivy picked up her cloth napkin, rubbing it along her lips to get the sticky soup off.

"What radio station do we listen to tonight? And who is old enough now for some wine?" Dod Yakov asked. Then he walked with his bad leg to the trolley and picked up the bottle of wine. His arms were still large, and strong, and he pulled out the cork piece easily with a pocketknife. Dod Yakov poured my grandmother some wine, then my mother, and me, finishing with Ivy, who brushed some fallen matzo crumbs over her knees and tried to look serious.

"We will be telling stories now! I will tell again to my nieces how I saved my own children when we had nothing to eat but bread and lemon juice," Doda Esther called out, walking back into the dining room with a serving knife and fork for the chicken.

"Yes, yes," Dod Yakov said and my sister pulled her skirt down.

"Aach, Yakov," Doda Esther began." Don't you remember our son Yaron came down with yellow fever during the war. And Ada says not to tell the girls any more stories; I will bore them. I walked all the way to Tel Aviv just to find him some medicine. This is identity; I tell you. You don't remember, Yakov?"

"Did you walk?" Dod Yakov asked, finally putting the wine bottle on the table." I don't think it was like this."

Doda Esther picked up a napkin and wiped her brow, tossing the serving utensils onto the table. "The Israeli soldiers in the jeep found me, but it was not for many kilometers, I tell you," she said. "There was not a drop of food in the whole house. I was picked up by our boys, and they took me into Tel Aviv. Ivy, and Liana—did I tell you the story of how once this house was so dark, we had to live only with candles? This was during the War of Independence, your mother was not with us, of course, she was in America where they play tennis all the time."

"Esther!" My mother shouted. "I did plenty in the war. Don't tell my daughters that I was in America taking naps!"

Lifting the dish of chicken, Esther indicated by one forefinger the circle the dish was to follow around the table, like a map.

"The women of Jerusalem, they are a powerful group of women," Zorah offered.

Doda Esther took a crusty breast onto her plate when it finally passed to her.

I studied Savta. She was searching for impurities and picking bad pignolia nuts out from on top of the baked chicken.

"So you begin the story for the night," Esther said. "Nu, Zorah? My sister has had her say for a little while now."

"Very well," Zorah said. "Okay, as they say in America." She lay down her fork pushed her plate of chicken away, and inhaled. "When the British occupied the streets long ago, they thought our grocer, Mr. Haggittee, was a bit strange. In his store, he sold magazines which were a—how you say? These magazines were for men alone, you say. Your grandmother was no spring chicken at this time, mind you—she had already five children. But, Mr. Haggittee couldn't keep his eyes off her. When the War of Independence against the British finally started, you could not even get a drop of lemon from the stores. Everything shut down—and Arab and Jew, not talking, killing. Mr. Haggittee would sneak to your grandmother's house with fresh food he had hidden for her. I am talking about cream, strawberries, wonderful big oranges that he went all the way to the farms in Jordan to get for her. He would climb to Savta's bedroom with all these things hidden in his shoes, his overcoat, under his hat. When the British saw him creeping up on Savta like this in the night, they thought he was a 'Peeping Tom,' and they shot one of his eyes off."

"Oy, Pee-pee Tom," Savta said." Oy, oy."

"I hear Savta still gets her rice from Mr. Haggittee's store, do you know, Liana and Ivy?" Zorah said. "Mr. Haggittee is quite famous you see for things that are a bit forbidden. Savta sends always someone to fetch what she needs from him for the Friday night meals."

"What's a 'Peeping Tom'?" I asked.

"They look at women, and they get excited by this looking," Zorah explained to me. "You have in New York many 'Peeping Toms,' I think. Yes, darling? The 'Peeping Tom' likes to sneak up on women when they are undressing, you see, Liana. Just to look is what makes the 'Peeping Tom' excited. And the women, they have no clothes on, you see."

"Oy, oy," Savta said louder, waving her hand. My mother had started laughing. Savta got up from her seat and took off the shawl she wore around her shoulders and quickly covered me, wrapping it around me.

I pulled Savta's shawl down over my shoulders and watched my grandmother as she struggled to sit again at her place on the table.

Esther leaned over and helped Savta find her fork again and the plate of chicken she had dished out from the serving platter. "This is not a nice story for the dinner table," Doda Esther said.

I looked away, into the unlit kitchen, then I imagined the old man who lost his eye climbing up from where the garbage pails were outside and the stray cats nested, to the second story. My grandmother's bedroom was once where Doda Esther's was.

"It was terrible, I tell you," Zorah said." Mr. Haggittee tells everyone that it was the war that took out his eye, but your grandmother has told me the real story."

"Mr. Haggittee—true believer in State of Israel," Savta said now, in her broken English.

"Oy, Zorah," my mother was laughing, "you are going make me make pee-pee in my panties!"

"What nightmares these girls shall have tonight," Doda Esther said.

"Mr. Haggittee got ill a few years later," Zorah went on. "And to this day never married or had any children after his eye was shot and he was put in prison on the false arrest. Your grandmother said he suffered this disgrace long ago poorly. She says he still keeps the British pornography books on the back shelves to prove to every customer that they were the real perverts the whole time." She took up her knife and began to cut into her chicken. She was tall and beautiful, I thought, like Savta—two beautiful women, and soft. "I hope to play cards with Savta this night," she said. "I have known your grandmother as long as I have known this life."

Dod Yakov lifted his yarmulke up from inside his napkin and felt to see if it were still wet. He put it on his head, with its blots of soup and liquid.

My grandmother nodded and smiled, her dentures glistening like white china plates.

"Now, I will tell you a story. It is my turn," Doda Esther said. "Do not think the British were so bad. We all went to British schools, and we were even in the same war together against Mr. Hitler. This War of Independence was something unusual; I tell you. So listen now. I walked openly in the streets to the concerts when the War of Independence broke out. You know the women—we carried ammunition in our brassieres to our soldiers in the underground. We would walk down the streets proud as peacocks, as if we were going only to the concert for the evening! We were not members of the Stern Gang. This you must know. The Stern Gang believed they were the real underground. They used to put bombs in people's cars. We knew the British were very much gentlemen and would not have stopped us."

"We have already heard this story. a million times, Esther," my mother said.

"We women of Metadulah Street had ammunition in our girdles and corsets when we walked through the village, and pretended just that we were going to hear a concert at the municipality," Doda Esther pushed on." We put Savta in the closet during the bombings. She would sit in a little wooden chair the size of a cooking pot and when I went to get her after all the noise, I would worry that she had fainted."

"Liana," Dod Yakov said, turning to me." Wouldn't you like a story about your grandfather?"

"Yes," I stared into the marks and swellings from his straw hat.

"My father always took me to parties in Trans Jordan," my mother blurted. "Your grandfather supplied the Middle East. We all had wonderful dolls and wonderful silver, dishes and things like that. That's why he used to go to Europe so much. My father used to take us when he went over there to buy for the store. He would photograph a Jewish and Arab woman each holding a Remington typewriter at the Wailing Wall for his store catalogue. During all the terrible riots, we still went to Mischanot to play our games of tennis with him. We played with floor brooms if we could not find our tennis rackets any more! Live and let live, my father would say."

"Wait," Yakov said. "Just wait and all this about the water and Jordan villages will die down. We will take you in the Ford to the borders, and I will point out to you where the old store was."

There was a long silence. The faces around me turned to their chicken and challah bread. I waited.

"Perhaps if I see Shraga again he will tell me where the old boats are kept," my mother said at last, looking up from her plate. "I don't like to go to Akko with Shraga when I visit Eilat. There, he runs a hotel now on the Red Sea. It still has that terrible smell, this is a terrible smell and I don't like this smell; it is terrible. You can see, too, the ropes are still hanging—I heard this story from Shraga. If it was serious what the young boys did in the underground—they would hang them. It was not always that the British knew who was serious and who was just a boy playing with balls, shall we say—and the British could also be very gentle and kind."

"I don't think the British wanted to be there," Doda Esther added softly.

"Well, you hear all these stories about the British," My mother coughed." But, the truth is they were very nice and would smoke with you and be very much gentlemen. Much more civilized than the army of both sides—the Likud and the Haganah were rough men you must remember. The Goyim are not very smart in general and they use the Jew for his know-how. I honestly don't think the British knew what to make of all of us there, but they were very polite and quite cordial. My father sent my brothers to British schools, and I was in London as a teenager and we marched in the rain against the 'White Paper' but to tell you honestly this paper I never really read. You know my boyfriends in Jerusalem would make so much out of it, but to tell you honestly, I see many of the Likud and Haganah soldiers now and it turns out some of them are a little bit idiotic—I even look at Shraga and say to myself: this man is a little bit of an idiot after all, what was he all about? I mean, really."

"Ada, really," Esther said," try to be serious for once, will you?"

"If you say Silberfeld to anyone in Jerusalem, they would know who we were," my mother went on." Because we had the largest store. My brothers, they would keep everything hidden in their Ford, and they would pass the British soldiers on their way to deliver it and they would say to the British officers: 'How are you today? And how is your wife? And would you like some of our household goods for your party this Saturday?' Most of my boyfriends now, from the Haganah, I hear run hotels on the Red Sea in Eilat or maybe in Tel Aviv. Perhaps they will come next week at the King David."

My mother pushed one of her hands around her head, flattening down her stiff, colored curls.

Doda Esther turned to Savta's friend. "Tell us about what is going on in Jerusalem at this very moment, Zorah. Do you not have a nephew in the IDF? He must have told you. Why are these soldiers in the street? Do you know some young soldiers came into my house today to ask me questions. Perhaps Zorah can tell us now what is going on around this place, as you Americans would say." My aunt loved repeating American catchwords, like my mother, which she also mispronounced or exaggerated. They got them from the shows of "Bonanza" and "The Untouchables" that came on the RCA TV from Lebanon.

"Essentially," Zorah began in a careful, clipped British pronunciation of English, "what is occurring is that they do not want us to build our water supply. And Syria is sending snipers and terrorists to the Jordanian borders around Jerusalem at this moment to prevent us from taking our water from the mountains. Not all the Jordanians agree with the Syrians you must know. And there is suspicion that the diplomat's son has been kidnapped as an act of defiance by the Syrian militants. I say, of course, only a suspicion."

Doda Esther cleared her throat. She whisked up 'The Jerusalem Post' off the trolly. "'On the far horizon, in the Kingdom of Jordan,'" she read melodramatically: "'negotiations continue for the Jerusalem Water Project' . . . This is today's Post." Esther folded the paper, gesturing it at our guest.

Zorah lifted up her water glass and took a sip of the flat club soda. "I hope our old Arab friends have deserted their summer villas by now, gone to Amman like the others. It is impossible to have them there. Our planes are over the dams the Syrians are building to stop the water from flowing to Israel as we speak this minute," she said. "And they will flatten these dams the Syrians are making."

My grandmother's eyes were closed, as if she were napping. Her mouth twitched slightly.

"Savta, *ma-shlo-ma*?" Doda Esther turned to see whether my grandmother was all right. Then Savta opened her eyes and smiled with the full set of her new white teeth.

I glanced away, into the kitchen again. From my chair inside the dining room, Carmela, the Yemenite maid's, feet looked like crabs. I watched her as she stooped and hoisted her tattered dress above the onion skins, peeled potato skins, and droppings that had been splattered all over the kitchen floor when Doda Esther was cooking this morning.

"Liana, sweetheart, are you feeling sick?" My mother asked. "I can bring you some cooled tea I have upstairs in the bedroom. I put a cup out on the upstairs verandah."

"Yes, but the tea will only stain the towels. It will make things worse; we will have to use more water to wash the towel off."

"Aach, Esther," my mother complained, "don't tell me about tea. I know about tea, Esther."

"I will tell you quite simply that the military director if the IDF is an idiot," Zorah continued. "Since he has been in office, we have these things that are nothing. Last year they followed a boy named Yoselle all the way to Brooklyn because they said he was kidnapped by Russian spies. Then it turns out this boy was kidnapped by his own father, an Orthodox Jew who hated everything here and wanted his son back from the mother who was a kibbutznik. A little too much James Bond, I believe. Double-O-Seven you say?"

"What do you hear of the new Chief of Intelligence from the Mossad?" Dod Yakov asked Zorah. " I knew Issar, Ha Gadol. Issar, the Big. The first Chief of Intelligence, did I tell you? We had thirty spies

back then, and most of us were only lawyers, accountants, pharmacists
. . . you know."

"Who is this boy that has disappeared?" My mother asked.

"They have announced it already twenty times, Ada, you do not listen? The son of the Charge D'Affaires, what is the matter with you?
His name is William Coons, a Junior." Doda Esther said.

"No, no. William Coons, Junior, Esther. I know English better than
you. All night they will tell this terrible story on the radio."

"It is not a story, Ada, now they call such things an incident. What
does this boy look like, do you think?" Esther asked.

"What? I know?" My mother said. "What do you think? He is a
friend of mine from Westchester?"

"If the diplomat's boy has been abducted by the Syrian militants,"
Zorah explained now, as if suddenly talking to children," the houses
along the bank here will be searched. And all borders going into Jordan, and Eine Gede will be blocked. So whatever things you would like
to do—shopping, etc.—I would suggest getting them done before-
hand." She picked at a tobacco-stained spot on her teeth, took out a
moist crumb of some sort. "So that we cannot have the Jordan River
supply, the Syrians shall build dams down by Eine Gede."

"What do you want from us, Zorah? I am not concerned with all
this." My aunt sucked in her chest. "I was an old woman very early in
life. I was in the Haganah as a girl younger than Liana. I am ten years
older than Ada as I have mentioned. And Savta was so tired after she
had her, I had to leave school to take care of her. This new generation
doesn't want to know what old Palestine was like."

"No one asked you to leave school," my mother protested. I watched
her press into some strips of bread she had shredded on the table.

"What do you mean?" Doda Esther shouted. "Finally, at age
twenty, when your mother is at last in the army, I went to Vienna to
study psy-kah-lo-gee. Did you know, children, your mother was born
on the kitchen table? But in the old city she was born, of course, as she
will tell you. We only have the table from the old days. There was no
food in the cupboards when the riots started in the streets. Savta

wrapped your mother quickly in blankets and brought her into the broom closet until the outside Jewish curfews were lifted and the streets of old Jerusalem were safe again. Perhaps next time she comes to Israel Liana and Ivy will go to the Ulpan like all the other foreign girls and learn Hebrew."

"Liana and Ivy are foreign?" My mother cried.

"Is there any dessert?" My uncle asked, weakly.

"Now, I will tell a story!" My mother picked up her wineglass, holding it up midair. She was growing excited. My mother was performing now. Telling us this story would soon prove to be a success of her deeper nature. Was she also showing us her rejection of the polite and proper suburban housewife, every bit worth discarding as the stiff curled edges of her pita? "I had a cousin who had a motorbike," she began. "This cousin would say to me: 'Do you want to go for a ride?' And I would know exactly what he meant. He gave me ammunition, and I put it under my skirt, inside my under panties. We drove through Jerusalem on his motorbike and onto the highway to Tel Aviv to deliver it. 'Til now people don't know we did it. You can't say we were heroes because I don't think we knew it was dangerous. You wanted the country, and you did as you were told. I take Liana and Ivy to Ramat Rachel, they will see where they put a rifle in my arms at their age, near the chicken coops. It was no joke, all of us girls with our rifles in this kibbutz. We slept in the bushes."

What we needed, my sister and I, more than anything else, was for her to go back to being just a housewife, an oddity. Not made into more of an enchantment to us. But, she held her eyes on Ivy and me. As if she really wanted to tell us it was like great sex—her underground—the best sex she had ever had. But, either she couldn't find the right words, or knowing the right words, was not about to come right out and explain it to us. "You know Savta was born in the old city. Savta's father was really the first doctor of Palestine, though really he was only a pharmacist."

"Oy, Ada," Doda Esther said, "you exaggerate, Ada. Maybe once you did this with the rifles."

"You weren't there," my mother said. "What do you know about what I did in the Haganah? Don't get them all mixed up."

"I get them all mixed up?"

"You know, everyone in Israel knows what we did," my mother went on. "I go to the King David Hotel and I am treated like I am a movie star."

"As you wish—"Doda Esther said.

"If it wasn't serious what the young boys of the Jewish underground did," My mother said, turning to look at Ivy and me, "the British would only beat the boys that they caught with their riding crops on the tookie."

"Ada really," Esther said.

"The English beat everyone. Liana, you know what a tookie is?" My mother asked, looking at me. "This is a tookie!" My mother stood up and swatted her behind with the flat of her hand. "Like this. One, two, three, four. Oh, but it hurts. You would like that?"

"Jesus frigging Christ," Ivy said.

"If you don't like this, then don't be an Israeli in the underground." Then, "Enough!" My mother said and waved her hand in the air.

But it wasn't enough.

"Well, then bend over, my darling," Esther cleared her throat. "I would be happy to spank you now," she said.

My mother jumped and lifted the hem of her sundress to her thighs, laughing.

"Ada-leh, no! For heavens sake, Ada-leh," Zorah howled.

"I will ask the maid to clear the table now," Esther said, yawning.

Slowly my mother lowered her dress tail, but she didn't falter or lose her composure. She fell back into her chair, and then looked up. "It is better if I go to sleep early tonight, Esther," she said. " I am very tired for some reason. This day, I'm afraid, has been quite a lot."

The evening came to Jerusalem from a limestone-heavy earth. At five o'clock, the next Friday afternoon I awoke from the afternoon siesta to the sounds of the first rain pellets hitting the glass doors to the upstairs bedroom verandah.

I lifted the stiff, hand-washed sheet and sat up on my cot. I was in a thin nightgown made of synthetic silk that I had bought in one of the dusty Jerusalem shops on Bezalel Street. I pulled up the ankle length gown, at its hem, and, holding it between two fingers, glanced over at my sister who was sleeping in her cot against the wall. The white sheets on Ivy's bed had been tucked and folded, and there was the lingering smell of her cigarette smoke in the air. It had settled on some of the clothes she left out of the closet, either from this morning, or from all the other times she smoked out in the garden with the neighbor's boy, a soldier. She had left her small transistor radio on, it was on her night table; the volume turned down low.

All the rooms in the pentagonal, sprawling house had yellow marble floors like this one, and wobbly doors with handles that were held together loosely, with bolts and screws that looked like broken, old teeth.

Yesterday, Ivy and I found a trunk filled with fake passports, old rolls of white lace, and dark dresses in the bedroom closet. I knew better than to ask my mother about it. She fell asleep last night, holding a cloth-bound album, her finger touching the picture of her brother Elizar again.

The metal blinds were up on the window overlooking Metaduleh Street. I felt the dangers of the outside roads again, the terror on the sensuous stones. Now I saw my mother's messy stockings on the floor, scattered in rolled up balls. She planned to wash when there was enough water in the bathroom. Her sandals lay askew on their tops with their street-soiled soles flipped into view. She was sleeping in her white nylon slip and girdle on her bed across the room by the door.

Doda Esther had laid a pail of water on the floor by my cot this morning. Leaning down, I dipped my finger into the warm liquid. The water looked slightly brown, undrinkable, as if Esther had slipped some mud in it when I was sleeping to make sure I wouldn't abuse my ration. The water I used for my sponge baths was boiled and given to the Yemenite maid, Carmela, to use again to wash the floors.

Wiping my finger on my nightgown, I got off my bed and went to the verandah doors to look out to the back of the house, the side not facing the street. It must have been raining all siesta while I was asleep. There wasn't a splashing of rain outside like in America where the downpours are rushing streams of sky-water, but a constant dripping, a hammering on the desiccated soils, together with the pale yellow glow of sun.

A wet wind came at my face. On the slightly opened glass doors, I saw the raindrops gliding down, clear and big. I strained to focus on the small garden underneath the second floor landing. The flowers smelled syrupy, like sweet blackberries in the wetness and heat. Skinny pine trees brought the only shade to the ledges of the back porches but beyond, towards the eastern hills, a vast, wild field and woods loomed. The trees in the garden looked drenched, and the ground had turned into a slosh of white mud. The distant field and stonescape were soaked, too.

I tiptoed to my sister's bed, picked up her radio, and listened to the English voice coming through its static. The news reports about the missing diplomat's son and a description of the same face I had seen in the photos at the airport was on the radio again. I had heard the army jeeps by the dormitory up the street very early in the morning. Reporters had come from Tel Aviv, and the border police patrolled the streets. The kharmsin, "very bad weather," was on its way—the unbearable heat wave that would sweep the country.

Everyday before siesta, I went down to the old grocery shop near the pharmacy. There wasn't a travel agency in sight. Tickets to the Egged buses were sold in the shop with warm bottles of Coca-Cola, and maps to Southern Eilat. I searched through the worn, dusty brochures and found faded guides to Europe, left over from the days before the War for Independence, when travel to other places was frequent and you could sail from Haifa to Italy. The railroad station was near the only post office. I now figured if I saved enough lira from the money. my aunt gave me to pick up eggs and milk, I could take the train to Tel Aviv, back to the airport. I still did not know how much it would cost then for an airline ticket to Paris, or, if I could cash in my return ticket. I had pulled it out of my mother's suitcase a few days ago.

Propped up under my mother's dressing mirror was the name of a ball-room at the King David Hotel where the party Doda Esther had spoken of was to be held tonight. The date: JUNE 30, 1963, was embossed in English with the time, seven p.m. My mother was taking Ivy and me to the King David, to the reunion and celebration of the first excavation of graves. The bones belonging to the Jewish fighters of The War of Independence against Great Britain had been successfully lifted out of the Jordanian cemetery this afternoon and were on their way by truck to the new Israeli grave site by the President's House for the ceremony taking place in a few days. Tonight, members of the old division of Jerusalem's Haganah— people who had been with my mother in the 1947 underground—were going to attend the party.

Quietly, I made my way to the bedroom door, and watching my mother through the corner of my eyes, opened the door and closed it behind me, leaving the room soundlessly.

Out in the hall vestibule, I tried to think. Yesterday and the day before I had sat with my sister on the couch here and watched the sunset out the window, the ephemeral lavender cloak. A certain beauty had enclosed us; it had made us quiet with one another. I thought of my father, half-believing that he would be sitting in some cafe on the St. Germaine Boulevard in Paris sipping cafe au lait, and would look up, recognizing me, and tell me this had all been some kind of bad joke. All week, my mother had pulled at Ivy and me with whispers. We were to "forget" my father's "accident" and "not speak of him in front of people here."

I went to a small oak cabinet near the window and pulled opened its top drawer. It brimmed over with documents in Hebrew, stubs saved from concerts in the new city and theatrical events, bus passes to the militarized territories with an official-looking photograph of my uncle Yakov on them, and, for some reason, pictures of stemmed flowers. I fingered one of the passes, reading:

This is not a free pass.

This pass is issued by the military commander solely for the purpose of entering the area stated on the front.

This pass can be withdrawn by the military commander at any time without giving prior reason . . .

I put it down and felt for loose change. The shiny surfaces of some silver English coins with pictures of Queen Elizabeth on them looked as big as tea saucers. I shut the drawer.

Slowly, holding onto the copper banister, I began my descent down yellow marble stairs that were slippery with cleaning fluids, and wound down to the first floor of the house.

In the foyer, I smelled the odors of my grandmother's sickbed in the air—a sweet medicinal odor, like cherry syrup, and alcohol. Savta must have turned on the lamp and then gone back to her bedroom. I could see her spectacles on the small table glinting under the foyer mirror. The house was full of odd reflections. In the early evenings hours you could feel the sweat of the hardworking dead, the laboring of ghosts. By the evening, with the cooling of the air and the moon looking like a floating turnip outside in the lavender sky, I could see my reflection in the shadows downstairs, from different places inside the house.

It had become almost second nature to me now, to walk through the late afternoon shadows, between the whitewashed walls, to tiptoe on the musty Arabic carpets in the glareless silence of the hours before anyone else woke from the siesta, opening private drawers and searching the furniture to find lira, to pocket what wasn't mine for Paris. In the dining room, I looked for loose money on the cabinet shelves and table. I didn't find any lira that evening.

The kitchen door was open, and I entered the clean room easily. Savta usually left some "grush," Israeli pennies shaped like silver starfish, for the delivery boy from Mr. Haggittee's on the kitchen table. I walked to the table, reaching up and pulling the long metal chain that was attached to the overhead lamp. The small bulb cast a yellow light over the scratched Formica. There was a bowl of fat Jaffa oranges on the table and a loaf of challah bread, but no change today.

I opened some sliding glass doors and stepped outside onto the kitchen's verandah. I went to a rusted lounge chair by the balcony and scooped out a tiny puddle of rainwater from the seat with the cup of my hand. I sat down in the chair, and I wondered if my mother was awake yet.

The puddle on the plastic seat seeped into my nightgown, the wind was starting up; the heat would be back soon. Bits of pine cones and wet pine needles stuck on the washed hosiery and sheets left out to dry last night, hanging heavy on the few clothespins Carmela had used on the twine. Underneath the porch was the garden where a leisure hammock hung between two trees in the shade.

I tried to shake off the drops of rainwater that slid down from the seat of the lounge chair to my feet.

My mother was in her element here, I thought, it was Israel and hot. Maybe she could be happy here, not need me so much. She could wear her tent dresses and walk barelegged, with her kerchiefs tied around her neck. She could decide dressing any morning that she was not in need of underpants, or any other undergarment. No one would care or judge her as they did in Katonah.

The setting sun was a broad, magnified flame, widening and, staring outward to the distant field and woods, I slowly summed up all the obstacles in my way to going to Paris: my mother, the stifling, coarse country that would watch everything I did as if we were in a police state somewhere, the fact that I had no more than a hundred dollars and a few lira saved, and beyond the garden, the small pine forest, and few Jewish houses, raw barbed wire made it impossible to skip off the property, and then go up further to the Jordanian hills. And though the wire was old now and weather-eaten, there were buried mines in the field beyond it.

Tottering, old warning signs and rusted barbed wire sectioned the formerly militarized territory full of gun shells and helmets and lizards.

Most of the Israelis didn't give into the fears about the Russians, as pilots were shown in Syria with Russian Migs and air-to-air satellites and charges were made on the BBC and American channels that Communists were behind the recent border disputes. The news in Jerusalem went on about the water, the fighting along the pipelines that carried streams from the Jordanian mountains and wadis, upwards into Jewish held territories.

The wind snapped at the hosiery line. I looked at another of my mother's broad girdles, hanging on one clothespin with several other articles of clothing. Somehow, from this perspective, it looked hexed by the warm rainfall, the fertile pine scents. It had dried and gotten wet again with the rain, its white fabric luminously spotted. Laundry soap and some of my mother's almond body wash had remained on the girdle sweating her hearty scents.

I turned away.

In the drizzling rain, the Jordanian hills seemed closer than when I tried to see them from the bedroom upstairs. They lay to the east, though named "The West Bank." The boundary between the Arab and Jewish regions was drawn by a fountain pen years ago when some British engineers came to canvas the rough land in the 1930s. The ink they had used was green, and so the border was called: "the green line," my aunt told me. The border had remained vague and uncertain, she said, subject to weather and other forces. No one ever seemed to know where it started or ended, the barbed wire often arbitrarily strewn to make up for the absence of clearness. A little more than a hazy outline still in the distance, there were thick layers of barbed wire, on both sides of the border.

I settled back into a daze, as if hopelessness were soon to become my state of permanence, too. I wished I had brought a package of the pink Israeli chewing gum down with me. Tears came and went, leaving a vacancy in my feelings.

Then, for a long moment, I lost track of myself and just floated, ghostlike, watching, blankly, the moistened trees.

Suddenly, I heard loud sounds in the distance, a noise treading in the small pine forest. Human movements usually tread slowly and cautiously in the woods. I got off the lounge chair which wetly sucked me back. I breathed in, feeling the faraway movements like a sixth sense.

There was a tiny latch to the gate and in my nightgown and bare feet; I traveled down the verandah's outside steps to the garden. And then, beyond, into the small forest, following the sounds.

The spindly pine and walnut trees shielded me from the downpour and offered up their branches in the cool, fresh, and watery wind. I stopped. In the distance, some bushes were pulled and pushed above the rain. It was boots I heard, sucking in the wet whitish mud.

Then I spotted scattered clothes in the pine cones—a small child's tee-shirt, a pair of colored shorts, torn and smelling like the donkey manure in the souks of the old city. I knew the stench from the night my mother took me behind Jaffa Gate, and the poor children with their scabby heads had made the air razor-sharp with the rank, painful smell.

My gown got caught on a pine tree branch as I stretched my sight to take in a large figure, the rain splattering on his yellow raincoat. He was carrying something in his arms.

"Hey—" The stranger discovered me.

He walked towards me, his boots sucking through the thicket. "Go get some water," He shouted." The boy fell."

Through lines of falling rain, I saw that what the stranger held in his arms was a young, dark-skinned Arab boy. The child's chin was pressed into the stranger's arm like a girl's.

"Where?" I said. "Water? Where?" I pulled at my nightgown, ripped where my breasts were and held it in my fingers. Then I stared into the stranger. He was big and wide as a door. His arms were larger than I had seen on any man before. He wasn't thin, but his face was drawn, a red-hued beard on its cheeks. He looked like he hadn't had anything to eat for days, his jeans loose around his waist. A pair of white gym socks showed where the rubber toes of his rain boots had been torn open walking through the rocks with the boy in his arms.

"Where did he fall from?" I asked.

Under the shifting light, the delicate body in his arms was stiff, the eyes closed.

"From one of the trees the older boys were throwing stones at. Look," He said. "He's out, but I think he's just dehydrated. He must have been lying on that branch already gone from the heat, and no one noticed. Then he must have fallen. After the other boys were gone. We just have to get him some water and get him up, and then he'll run back. He'll be scared of us. Go on. Fill the bottles. They're some by my gear." He kneeled and put the boy down in the leaves.

The half a dozen empty milk bottles stood next to a huge duffel bag. I went and took a bottle up. Then I ran out into a clearing, where there weren't any tree branches, holding the bottle out, up to the rain. I heard my heart pounding over the drumming of the raindrops. My hands were trembling. Raindrops dribbled into the bottle. Milk left at its bottom made the water turn a translucent white. I tried to hurry, but the stranger didn't call me back. A sudden wind from a distant hill sent some pine needles swerving into the bottle with the rain, so I stuck my finger into the bottle's mouth and tried to spade them out.

Then I walked backwards over to where the stranger had lain the stricken boy. He was kneeling over him, under the branches of one of the trees. I turned and faced the child's smooth skin, the color of the light brown leaves. His body no more than a slit under the stranger's.

"Can you give me the bottle?" The stranger asked.

I held the bottle up and said: "There's some pine needles in there, I tried to get them out."

"A little pine juice won't hurt him," He said.

"I should get more." I said.

"It's almost stopped raining. This will have to be enough." He turned back to the child. "Here boy, open up," he said. "Drink some of this."

That was when I recognized who the stranger was. His hair wasn't in a crew cut anymore. It had grown out, unkempt and scary, but I recognized him. He was the American in the photograph the marshal had held up to me at the airport. The diplomat's son. The one I had been hearing about all week. Only he wasn't much of a teenager, he was eighteen, or twenty. Under his raincoat, I saw a huge button that read: "R.O.T.C., Fourth Division" pinned on. He had the same reddish auburn hair as my mother, but the strands of his hair were too straight, as if washed too much in the Israeli soap and hard water. He was also freckled and fair like her, but he was distinctly un-Israeli and his beard gave the rest of his broad body a mature look. His eyes were so small,

I couldn't tell what color they were.

The rain was stopping too abruptly. He was pulling at the child's eyelids, and suddenly the boy's eyes were rolling, alert. The stranger lifted up the curly head and made him drink some of the water.

"Baaa-sss—" the boy finally screamed. He hit his own head with the heel of his small hand.

The stranger helped him stand up. He held the naked, thin shoulders between his two fists. But, the child didn't like being roused. He tried to hit himself again and the stranger grabbed hold of his arm. The boy yanked it away. Then he ran off, raced on like a mouse, away.

Now the stranger rubbed his hands on his jeans. He walked to a rock and sat down. His boot nudged at a pile of moist dirt and leaves. His large toes muddied, and he just sat there unaffected, undisturbed, as if he couldn't feel it, the seeping of the white mud into his soles." I hope we helped him," he said." Jesus. It's his life, but I saw him fall."

"You did?"

Powerful he sat, a bewildering mix of tenderness and danger. "What should we do about his clothes?" I asked.

The stranger took out a pack of cigarettes and began to smoke. "I know who you are," I said, revealing myself to him." I saw your picture."

"Are you American?"

"My mother's Israeli, but I'm an American."

"Who else saw my picture?"

"I don't know," I said. "It was at the airport. Some kind of police-man showed it to me."

"My name is Williams Coons," He said. "I was on my way out of Jerusalem. And then, it started to rain. Then I saw the boy. I don't know what he was doing. I thought it would be too wet to keep walking anyway." In the twilight, the stains that the white mud and crushed leaves had made on his clothes glowed.

"Not much time until it gets too dark to see out here," he said. "I think the military police might comb this place soon. They're looking for the Arab children, too. The older sons. There've been some skirmishes at the borders here. The older boys have guns."

"What will you do if the police come?"

The stranger looked down at the spot where he had mashed out his cigarette and sighed. "Oh, I don't know," he said. "I'd figure it out." In his eyes was this kindness that made him seem sort of lost. "What're you doing in Israel?" He asked. "Did you come to live with your mother?"

"No. She's been in America for a long time."

"I'm sorry," he said. But, then his eyes probed into mine. "Promise you won't tell the police."

"I promise."

"Who else lives with you?"

"Just my aunt And my grandmother, then there's my uncle, and my sister—"

He laughed. "That's a lot there."

"I won't be here long," I said.

"You won't?"

"No, of course, not." I turned and touched the bark of one of the pine trees; a gesture of rubbing against the roughly-edged and moist wood began in my hand.

"Look, isn't it beautiful here?" He asked after some moments passed. "The houses on the rocky hill up there behind the barbed wire all have terraces filled with birds. I've seen some black feathered ones, but I don't know exactly what they are. I don't know if they're sparrows like in America. Before the war, those houses were full of people. The people went over the Jordanian mountain rift a few miles away, just kind of deserted them all."

"What's over the rift?" I came closer to where he sat, my nightgown clinging to my thighs and legs in its wetness. But, I stopped before I got too close to him. And stood stiffly.

"Jericho is down there, where the water is. The Dead Sea. Some tents, I think, shepherds, hell, I don't know. Maybe nothing. I haven't been there. My father was stationed here."

"What's here?"

"Here? Well, I mean Israel."

He took out another cigarette and lighted it with a silver lighter he pulled out of his bluejeans. His head was tipped forward so that a shadow fell on his prominent nose. He was not old yet but he was not young either. He and I might have been brother and sister in the sense that two white-skinned teenagers had wandered into some foreign field where children with cloudy genders lie up in trees and then fall like human raindrops to the ground. Only to go running off naked and squealing. And fighting you.

"Are you sure you don't know who else saw my picture?" He asked after a few minutes.

"Of course I am," I said.

"Don't panic. You can't know how grateful I am to see another American. And the rain has made things cool down."

In the dampness, the coil at the end of his cigarette looked like a tiny red eye. The misty air absorbed his smoke rings, his exhalations. If I could walk into the center of him, my turn to be rescued might be waiting.

"The boy was just frightened," he said.

My nightgown was soaked. I could see through the white material of its torn skirt to my bellybutton. The stranger had some leaves in his fingers and he wiped his bluejeans off with them, he wiped his wrists and hands, and brought some up and wiped his neck. I copied him, bending and gathering up a handful of the smooth walnut leaves on the ground. They smelled good and sweet, and I wiped down my legs and wrung my hands with them, staring into the layer of clayish soil that came off as I wiped.

He threw his to the bushes when he finished, and then I threw mine.

"Jesus." His face widened, his smallish eyes gave it the effect of a face swollen with emotion that peaked and threatened its own flesh. "We were in Chile for a while." He looked up at the wet sky. "We're always stationed where we don't belong. You're lucky your mother's an Israeli. It must have been beautiful here before the war, even this field. I've seen some of the deserted Jewish homes, too, in the old quarter where the British had their elaborate villas full of gardens and terraces."

"Did they have birds, too?"

"Well, sure. I'm sure they had birds too."

"It's summer in America now," I said, one of my hands floating up to my hair, nervously." I miss it there."

"It would be interesting, though, to know what kinds of birds once flew through here," he said, as if he hadn't heard me. "It must have something once, Palestine."

The hem of my nightgown touched the mud. I watched as a new stain spread. I cracked off a pine branch, brushing off some wet dirt under my chin.

He got up from the rock, lifting up his huge hands as if trying to grab onto some invisible hold in the air, and I saw, finally, that his eyes were a bluish gray. "So, are you going to tell them? Are you going to tell the police?"

I shook my head at him, no.

He pulled back the sleeve of his tailored shirt, a softly ironed shirt like prep school boys wear, his high school R.O.T.C. medal on the starched lapel.

He went to his duffel bag, extinguishing another cigarette, and hoisting the bag up over his shoulder, then came back to where I stood.

He checked his watch. His eyes remote and removed, his head might have been a tower inside which his feelings lay waiting to be considered in private, either in a kind of consecration, or in self- crucifixion.

I let the pine branch drop from my hand. His expression began to frighten me again." I better get back," I said.

"Wait," he said. "Just be still for a second, if you want to see those birds I mean." He spoke in warm tones as he tugged open the duffel bag. He took out a blanket, whipping it into the air, then laying it on the leaves. The night flies had begun to make busy sounds in the pine trees, there was an old cat scratching at a shrub, the pine bark still oozing rainfall.

I watched when William squatted, straightening the corners of the blanket. First he kneeled. He dropped to one hip, then rolled back. His hands locked behind his head, like a man who did not expect to get any sleep for a long while. His weird eyes looked out— watching the places behind the border of barbed wire, the desolate Arabic houses on the hill—seeing if the boy would come out. I walked over and stood closer to him. I watched the distant houses with him. I stood in the leaves, switching my weight from foot to foot. The sky was darkening steadily, but he didn't want to talk much. Neither did I. The rain ran again, but it was lighter as we were together, just a drizzle, and we both opened our mouths and laughed when it ran into our faces, onto our tongues. The blanket became pleasantly moist, but the great mass of trees prevented it from getting soaked. No lights went on inside the houses on the hill for what felt like a good long time, and no sounds came from them, either. And then, the rain finished, stopping again. I never got down on the blanket beside him, but kept close. I was standing in the leaves watching when William sat up and raised his eyes and after a long while had passed said, "Does anyone know you're out here in your bedroom clothes? Isn't one of your folks going to come running to get you soon? It's getting dark."

"No one will come," I said.

William closed his eyes then, and from either lack of any food or the tiredness that finally overwhelmed him, fell into a happier state of rest, though not yet sleep. I did not want to stir him, or get too close to him. He must have been running for a long time. His face, under the first stars, looked pale. His size and strength were diminished making him safer to be near. It wasn't long before I saw William go out, fall hungrily into his missed sleep.

I looked at my watch. It was almost six-thirty. William was better under his trees with some of the night birds that he liked above, and sleeping hard enough for someone who must have been running for days now, without food or rest. Two birds on a low branch just above his eyes were watching him. They were enough.

I picked up my nightgown at its skirt, and tried to remember the path back to my grandmother's house, hoping my mother had just awakened from her siesta and would not be looking for me yet.

The cool of the evening was growing. The wind started up towards a darker night. I was searching for a path in the thistles when I saw the shadows moving amid the bushes and outlines of the trees. I stepped out of the path, back into the shrubs, and hid.

A small group of soldiers were approaching a clearing in the forest cautiously. One finally held up one hand, listened, then threw down his duffel bag about ten yards from me. I couldn't tell whether they were Israeli or Jordanian, the sun had disappeared and a long black cloak had blanketed the sky. Another soldier went behind a rock. I heard him urinating into the scorched grass.

I slipped more deeply into the bushes.

The rest of the unit stopped and took off their gear, and drew warm bottled orange sodas out of their duffel bags. I smelled apples and white cheese. The insignia pins on their berets glistened like gaudy baubles in the beginning moonlight. The air filled with thick cigarette smoke and laughter. They smoked more of their hand-rolled cigarettes and drank more orange soda.

From one of his pockets, a soldier pulled out a wooden recorder and began to play. The instrument made a hollow, sweet, and sharp sound, rougher than I would have heard in other places. Then I heard the screams.

Hurling across the steamy air came a raining storm of stones. "*Lo, lo!*" The soldiers shrilled in Hebrew. "*Me shama! Me shama!*" Walkie-talkies from their belts flashed and clicked like grenades or fat lizards, green and metallic in the hands of angry men.

Yards away, the rustling of their attackers sounded like snakes slinking back into a holed hiding-place under the leaves.

"*Shama.* Up there," the soldier with his pants not quite buckled shouted to the others. The other soldiers had out their guns, most eyeing the distant watchtowers on the Arabic side of the border a few hundred yards from where we were. Another one shouted:

"*Yallah!*"

Three of the soldiers had spotted a shadow high up in a large walnut tree not thirty yards away, across the grass. One tall soldier aimed. Two fired. I looked up, towards the small forest, back up to William.

A burst of gunfire blasted from the shadows in the walnut tree and shattered the wilderness.

The uniformed soldiers shot back, and I lunged behind the ridged mantle of a huge rock in the bushes. The volley of rounds deafening.

Then a silence came.

Up through white smoke and sparks, I saw some of the soldiers wiping at the thick dust on their faces. Then they took off running down the slope. Just as I saw the last indistinguishable uniform vanish beyond a mound of thistle and cactus, I heard branches snapping in the distant walnut tree. Two snipers were shimmying down its trunk. I saw their dark faces, their bare feet. They crouched, looking down, in all directions, then they skirted up the hill, to the barbed wire demarcation and the Jordanian fields. Their red-checkered keffiyehs unwrapping like streamers in the wind.

My mother was waiting for me. But, I was frozen behind the rock. I stared into the clearing where the others had been—the soldiers and gunfire. Only the clouds of their pleasure were left now, the billows of cigarette smoke, overturned bottles of soda.

Then something thudded to the ground, crying out. A flash of pale limbs sprawled across the path. If not for his nakedness, I would not have recognized the child William and I had fed with rainwater. His penis and his opened eyes drew me to him, though I didn't want to see him. His mass was no heavier than a broken melon fallen into the dirt and crushed, watery and string-like, moving in blood. That was when I saw the boot prints. Dozens of them in the path spread out like the face a clock. The prints on the ground cried out, too, showing a cross-fire. Gunshots between half a dozen half-blind Israeli soldiers and the slender Jordanian snipers had hit the naked child. He had tried to race up some tree to save himself. Did the soldiers even know they hit him? Did the snipers? Was that why they fled?

I crawled out from the shrubs.

I was moving to the child when as a flame violently blown away, he went out of this life, as removed from whatever, and all that had gone before as a stain.

I could not faint now, I thought. But, I tumbled into the leaves. I was the small child in the dreams that came. People from my past wandered in, knocking on doors. I saw the furry caterpillars on the Westchester trees, the woods where his accident rolled my father back to me, leaking blood. My English teacher from seventh grade was there, and my closest girlfriend, Sally Noakes. The cigarettes the soldiers smoked in the clearing turned into plumes of the narcotic brown hashish Ivy once brought into the woods with us back in Westchester, then suddenly my mother was coming from behind the intoxicating clouds to tell me. the school bus was ready for me at the end of our gravel driveway. When the final knock came, the one that opened the door from which I had fainted and fallen into the leaves, I recognized William's smell.

"Hush. Keep it low."

I made a violent mental effort to understand what was happening. The ground was cold and the wind fierce. My nightgown had been blown up to my waist. I felt William tugging it down. Then I was warm.

When my eyes looked above, William was holding me, and the moon was so white it looked like a floating bone. "Uh," he said. "Uh-uh— uh—" Then: "Jesus, Lord." The pupils of his gray eyes dilated, jolted. "It was an accident. When they were shooting at each other, the kid was up another tree. Between the soldiers and the sniper. A bullet caught him in the chest. I couldn't even tell which side. He was shot— Listen now, I took his bloody body—I buried him under some leaves in the forest. The Israeli military police will find him sooner or later. It's all I could do. They're looking for me. I'll put out my white handkerchief on the spot. They will have to see the handkerchief, and they'll find him. I think I took him to a good place. I hope I did—bring him to a good spot—"

The wind died down. I felt its last few breaths, its last licks, the last of the violence that shook the trees.

"Take my rain boots and we'll walk you back. Your feet will get cut." William pulled off his boots. His eyes strained to steady themselves. "You were out. Fainted. Give me your hands. No. One by one."

He wanted to help me balance on the leaves.

I leaned into him, wiping my feet, then I tried pushing them into the gigantic boots but I couldn't.

"No, no," William said. " They're too big. I'm going to carry you." William cleaned the blood from his hands on his jeans. He slipped his feet back into his rain boots and slung his duffel bag across one shoulder, before taking me up into his arms.

Then he carried me as he had the boy, trudging along the path in his rain boots, my head was under his chin and his hands tucked under my legs. I felt his breathing chest pillowing me as he exhaled.

I heard some dogs barking from the deserted aqua-blue Arab villas. But, we were quiet with each other.

Gun shells and corroded pieces of metal had been ground into the soil. Under the scorched desolate field were the bones of the dead, giving us a floor to walk on.

We walked downhill in almost total darkness.

He had to risk a candle in the final stretch of path, putting me down for the minutes it took to pull one out of his duffel bag and light one. I carried the candle in one hand after he lifted me back into his arms again. We waded through the shrubs and vines.

"That's your house there, isn't it?" William asked when we reached the anemones and white daisies, the hammock on my grandmother's property. He gently put me down, onto the ground, let me slip one leg at a time. I didn't speak, feeling his shoulder in the palms of my hand.

Then, opening the catch on the door, I let myself back inside the house, alone. His figure disappeared up the hand-laid limestone, back to the field. The empty kitchen was dark, and I stumbled to the hanging light bulb over the kitchen table, reached up and managed to pull the string that turned the light on.

I cried, burying my head in a kitchen towel, trying to remember the smell of the boy, his scattered clothes by the tree, the pine-scented rainwater. Not my father in the pool of blood and metal. But, I felt as if an hourglass had been turned upside down, the sand pouring out the minutes of lost grief as I felt my father slip through the edges of this darkness.

The air was hollow. My mother had not been in the kitchen. It had none of her fragrances. I did not hear her voice. William had held the boy, held me, both clammy slavers of blood and bones. At what point did that win over my mother's spell?

A cloud began to cover the still rising moon. The shadows of the bushes and pine trees floated silently through the pain in my head as I calmed. Now I had a friendship. William's arm.

I cleaned my hands with some napkins on the kitchen table and then stuffed the napkins into the rusted aluminum can under the sink. There were some raw chicken parts and livers inside clear glass bowls under the faucet, marinating in my aunt's lemon and sea salt and the humidity of the stone kitchen. I felt a fever on my cheeks.

When I walked inside the bedroom upstairs, the room was empty. My mother's bed had been left unmade, but her things had been moved around, piled into a new combination of sloppiness, her makeup left open on her dresser and her hairbrush with fresh auburn strands in its bristle.

I peeled off my torn nightgown. I wiped down my bare feet with another towel, from the bedroom closet.

I pulled on a denim wrap-around-skirt from a chair, slipped into my pair of white Bonwit Teller sandals and stockings, and buttoned up my blouse with its bumblebee on the pocket over my left breast, thinking of William.

I rushed back down the yellow marble stairway.

In the foyer, my grandmother's short-wave radio was turned on: "We interrupt our BBC programming," I heard a reporter say. "To update information received regarding the disappearance of the American Charges D'Affaires' son, William Coons. There have been unconfirmed reports that he was seen on the West Bank this morning . . ."

I picked up my mother's note, placed against the telephone on a small table with a china bowl of wrapped chocolates, hard candies, and my grandmother's spectacles. I read quickly:

"LIANA DARLING—

DID YOU FORGET WE MUST GO TO THE PARTY TONIGHT?

WE DID NOT FIND YOU WHEN WE WOKE FROM SIESTA. WE WILL MEET YOU AT THE BUS STOP AT 8:30.

PLEASE DON'T BE LATE.

YOU KNOW, DARLING, WHERE THE BUS STOP IS. I SHOWED YOU WHEN WE WENT TO TOWN LAST WEEK.

MOMMY."

By the clock, it was eight-thirty-six. I would be late.

3

"LIANA!" My mother shouted from the Egged bus shelter, looking heavier, plumper. Angry that I was late.

Ivy stood apart from her, smoking a Chesterfield.

My garter belt felt lumpy under my skirt, and I had pulled on two kinds of nylons. One was white and the other sheer, but I raced to them.

Soon, the bus came down from around the winding corner near Mr. Haggittee's grocery shop and, numb, I got on it.

As the bus doors closed behind us, my mother found a seat near the front. Ivy, dressed in her tight blue dress, walked to the back of the bus and climbed into the last row of seats.

I looked at Ivy, already settled into a back seat away from us, and smiling.

Out the bus window, the buildings were white as the moon while in the moonlight; their courtyards of hedges and flowers, flamed blue and red. I was not sure of anything more than the sudden and labile moods of the air and light. I yearned for William now.

Thin night clouds, like closing doors, had put the sun's fierce glare away, as if it were one of the dresses in the closet at Metaduleh Street. The evening moon showed its strength—its saucer-like; emblematic self so remote over a land made only drier by its unrequited thirst.

The bus turned up a broad street, and, in a few minutes, made its first stop in front of the International Dormitory of Hebrew University. Three or four army jeeps were parked at its entrances. "Shame to Jordan *ha Yom*! Shame to Jordan today!" someone was screaming down the limestone sidewalk. Israeli soldiers were clustered around the dormitory's doors. Vespas and Hondas, the foreign student's motorbikes, were chained to street lamps. A thick crowd of students milled around the police and green jeeps.

I ducked away from the poster of William on the billboards. It was an enlargement of the kind of photograph you see in high school yearbooks. Not different from the photograph the police officer had showed me at the airport. "Missing" was printed in English and Hebrew letters, with a telephone number added.

The engine gave out a roar right under me as the bus took off again, traveling faster up the street. A few yards away a police station lay, up Ben Yehuda Street, in the opposite direction.

I shifted and straightened.

There was something William had left for me in the night clouds. The tenderness that rose in me startled me. I would not tell the police what happened, or my mother. If I told my mother she would go to the station on Ben Yehuda Street, report the child's death, and I would never see William again. I would have to stay with her at Metadulah Street. Was I certain so early that this missing man would be my guide to a whole different set of reasonings and responses?

"Do you want to go shopping again tomorrow?" My mother waved back at me with her hand." I know this has been hard for you. Tonight, it is all my old friends, you know."

"Yes, Mom," I said.

"It's a lot to ask of you but please, I am a little lost still, Liana. Forgive me. We're going to have to get some sunglasses tomorrow. Put it on the list. Just a while longer and we'll be at the hotel." My mother kept tapping her fingers against the rim of the seat in front of her. She was anxious, anticipating the party with her old friends, clinging to her small formal evening purse. She had the same Kleenex in her hand she had used at the bus stop to wipe down her face, and her arms were big under her cardigan. She gazed out the passenger window at the old city. Hadn't whatever lay behind those ancient walls been her first home, too?

"Did you say something, Liana?" She turned to me again. I shook my head.

We were moving to the center of the new city, traveling up the stately boulevard called: King George Street stopped at a wide intersection girded by a Dutch windmill and a stone YWCA. Streetlights had already been turned on along the new avenues. A few modern traffic lights blinked. The billboards out the window advertised American movies: "Cleopatra" and "James Bond" holding a Colt 45 pistol, dressed in a tuxedo, and puffed white shirt. I looked out the bus window, wondering if I would be able to tell whether William was back at our special place in the field yet. I was on the other side of the border. On a Jewish street. The no-man's land behind my grandmother's house was just a distant mass of hills and rocks.

Minutes later, the bus reached the hotel.

The King David Hotel stood under the evening moon, its cup pattern of Jerusalem stones like marble baby cheeks. Two large cypress trees flanked its entrance.

The bus left Ivy, my mother, and me at the front door.

"Here we are, please . . ." My mother said. A doorman held the big entrance doors of the hotel open for all of us, ushering us in.

"*Todah, yeled*. Thank you, boy," my mother said to the waiter once we were seated in reserved seats by an indoor palm tree.

The waiter put down a bowl of crackers and roasted watermelon seeds and the Israeli white goat cheese and left us. I looked around the high-ceiled ballroom, to a performing stage where some of the band lounged under circles of flood lights, illuminating their garish trousers and jackets. A few soldiers hovered on wooden stools at the bar; their berets tucked under loops sewed on the sleeves of their green uniforms.

Most of the other guests had arrived before us and were sitting at their tables. They looked different from the Americans in the lobby.

"I cannot believe it!" My mother cried. "It's Tzivieh!" She stood up excitedly, and screamed, waving to a table where she had spotted an old friend from the Haganah, another muscular woman with a full head of black hair. I watched her rush to the table where Tzivieh sat. The women were in simple, dull dresses a few years behind the styles in America, and some of them had conspicuously giant plastic-rimmed eyeglasses with yellowed, thick lenses. A few wore their 1948 school dresses, the ones they had worn during their years in the underground, hand-sewn with embroidery on the chests, the fabric old with must and spots. The open shirts of the men were like those of the waiters, modern but made out of crude fabrics, polyester, too ironed, their trouser creases crisp enough to be paper.

My mother came back to our table, her face flushed and excited. She tried to take her seat again. But, suddenly, Ivy and I found ourselves surrounded by these older women, bending to extend kisses to our mother's cheek.

"Liana, this is Tzivieh," my mother said, her arm around the waist of one of these women.

I looked up at the chandelier in the center of the domed ceiling, its glass icicles were like cuts of a raw onion, and rough like the ones in the lobby.

My mother threw down a cocktail napkin she had ruffled in her hand. "*Ma shlo-mech*," she said, speaking so loudly the chandeliers seemed to shake. The women dispersed, and then a man with a black mustache and blue polyester trousers appeared at our table. My mother slapped playfully at his cheeks.

I leaned back in my chair and watched her—at this moment, in time, she was the center of attention, charismatic, turned on like the old chandeliers and dazzling among an embracing entourage, who, with their tough leathery faces, looked like a bunch of old outlaws. Even now, dressed in their responsible citizen clothes—teachers or lawyers, doctors, or businessmen—they still carried that criminal look, a lawless abandon.

"Now, a little refreshment!" My mother shouted into the air, finally seating herself, lifting a napkin up to place on her lap. Waiters had arrived from the sides of the ballroom with trays filled with dishes of food and wine bottles. Into the steamy air of cocktails and accordion music came the smell of olive oil and lemon.

When I looked back, only Tzvieh was standing by my mother's side. "Tzivieh," my mother said, patting the chair next to her. "Beh-vaka-shah, nu?"

"Do you know how long ago it was that your mother and I were in school together?" Tzivieh asked me. Thick circles of rouge sat on her cheeks, and she wore a necklace of black pearls. Tzivieh extended her hand to me, formally, with a great deal of muscle and robustness. I shook it quickly. She had put a hair band in her hair, the band of a young girl, one she might have worn herself long ago and her large feet barely fit into her high heels, which were decades old. "I am afraid my husband is no longer alive." She set herself down in a chair opposite me that my mother had placed her hand on. "And I have not kept up with enough friendships to find myself comfortable at any other table. But, I adore your mother you see."

"Tzivieh," my mother said, "these are my daughters, Liana and Ivy. Are you hungry, girls? It will be quite a party."

Ivy was pulling at her mascared eyelashes with her pinkie and thumb.

"Here we are!" My mother cried. "Liana, sit up straight. Put a napkin on your lap."

The waiter then put a basket of pita bread on the table from his tray, and an opened bottle of sweet wine with a plain white label on it, marked in some kind of Hebrew script. He laid a dish of sesame paste laden with oil on the center of the table and, cleaning off some white porcelain plates with a cloth napkin he drew from the hip rim of his trousers, set the table for the four of us. My mother's eyes became large.

I inhaled the odors of the bread and sesame spread. Paprika and salt clotted into thick clusters by the running oil. The fragrances began to intoxicate me. I found myself strangely calm, as if my heart were being soothed by the crusty faces around me, and my body becoming lighter. The shock of the boy's end in the leaves had sharpened all my senses. I saw my mother differently, heard her loud voice as sounds barking away at deeper desperations and losses. Then it was as if my keeping silent about what had happened in the forest was suddenly a way to be part of the things here, too, a way offered to me now as a gift, through scents and flavors, the hints of my mother's past.

The waiter poured us each a glass of mineral water and placed a huge bottle of blackberry syrup to flavor it.

"*Todah! Yoffee!*" My mother shouted at him, pulling at his sleeve. With a smile on his face from her touch he walked away, to the dance floor.

Ivy and I eyed the platter of lumpy sesame paste. There were no utensils to eat it with. We watched my mother break a slice of pita and scoop out some of its bread. She whisked up a ball of the paste with the edge of the bread now made into a kind of cracker and began nibbling and chewing and swallowing, wiggling in her seat with delight.

"*Yoffee, achshav.* Wonderful now," Tzivieh said.

"Come on, Tzivieh-leh," my mother said, playfully. "Could anyone understand the feeling of being in our underground?" She watched Tzivieh take up a ball of sesame paste in some pita she, too, carved out. "Never before did I think there were a place and time where if only for a short while I really belonged, and I didn't want to be anywhere else. I only wish my daughters know this feeling?"

I searched for a fork, lifting my plate. There were none.

"When we breathed, we breathed together. Did we not, dear Tzivieh?" My mother took a sip of her plain mineral water and curled her fingers around the lip of her water glass, flushing a little. "Oy," she said, putting down her pita and it's newly dipped up blob of sesame paste. "Look how fat I am getting, would you believe I was ever a slim teenager in the Haganah."

"It becomes you," Tzivieh said eagerly. "But I have seen pictures of you when you were young. You were always very round, no?"

"I was only in Westchester for a short part of my life, Tzivieh. My brother Elizar was quite a hero to me."

"Of course."

"You know my brother wanted to go to America. To California, to study to be an engineer. But, he had a terrible 'accident.'" My mother was staring at me.

"Yes, Ada, I remember," Tzivieh said.

My mother sighed, but she was still staring at me. I reached into my pocket to find a Kleenex to wipe my face. Was she testing my alertness? Did she know something had happened to me?

"I was in the Haganah before my sister Esther," my mother said, finally looking away from me, back at Tzivieh.

"Yes, of course. But is she not older than you?" Tzivieh asked her. My mother lifted up her glass of mineral water and took another large gulp. Then she started coughing, flagging her hand. "Should I hit you on the back, Ada-leh?" Tzivieh asked.

"No, no. I am fine." Her eyes were red and teary. "I am having too much fun remembering the past, but my daughters think I am a crazy person."

"You are enjoying your stay? Giveret Silberfeld?"

A short man asked, coming to our table. He bowed to my mother. "Yes, wonderful," my mother said.

"*Enee* Omi, remember?" The man was saying. "Ada, it's Omi. Will you please dance with me? You have been in America, this is right?"

I watched my mother on the dance floor with the stranger. A fierce and upbeat rendition of Hava Negilah began on the shiny ivory-keyed accordion. The electric guitar players picked it up, and then the drummer. There were others clapping on the shiny dance floor, singing and dancing. The drums pounded, and a tambourine clanked.

I pulled my hand out of my pocket and lifted up my cocktail napkin, staring at the emblem on it, a transposed photograph of the Israeli national flag, a tiny dark blue and white cloth. It had a slight aroma, like walnuts. Putting it to my lips, I took a taste of it, licking the edges.

Then the lights went on over the platform stage where the gaudily dressed band members now stationed themselves at their instruments: ready to play a set with electric guitars, accordions, and drums under some makeshift floodlights from a kibbutz. Soon, the waiters were clearing out the center of the ballroom, taking off vases and fold-up tables and chairs, exposing the bare shiny dance floor.

"Hava Neh Ranna . . ." My mother shouted from the dance floor a few minutes later, the short man's arms around her waist. She clapped her hands, held them high over her head. Clapped them twice more. The chandelier lights were bright as stars over her head, and my mother tossed her flats off and unlatched her stockings from their garters, rolling them all the way down to her ankles, and yanking them off.

"God damn," Ivy said, sniffing at the air. "What's that stink all of a sudden? You smell it?"

"What smell?" I said.

"It stinks in here."

I could feel my blush. "I don't smell anything."

"Come on, Liana," Ivy said. "Let's go the bar. I don't have to watch her make a fool out of herself."

My chair squeaked.

Ivy crossed the vast, manicured floor, making her way straight to the bar. I kept myself close against the wall, so I wouldn't be noticed. Scents of body sweat, and perfumes from the dance floor swept over me in waves, but I could also hear loud voices, the tinkling of glasses coming from the lobby where the tourists sat.

I put my hand against the thick wall, the solidness of its wood then conspired with the distance and gave me a sense of security, of reassurance. I was still a tourist, like the people in the lobby, I told myself. It wasn't too late to forget about everything, William and the Arab boy, was it? I still could go to Paris and be like the tourists tomorrow. My mother would be like them again sooner or later too. Tonight she was different, but it will rub off, and she will go back to the Westchester housewife she was, back to the way things were.

My sister had arrived at the isolated island of hanging wine glasses and sultry lighting and climbed onto a wooden stool at the bar counter far from my mother and the dining tables. Her profile was sharp, in opposition to my mother's, her chestnut hair a wall as it fell over her shoulders when her back was turned. The violet in her short dress looked deeper under the bar lights, the color of tulips. Her efforts at containment and control gave her flesh lines and creases early in life. Ivy could fold and seal herself inside her face; her face was like an envelope bearing the rest of her. Three or four young soldiers were mingling there at the bar.

"We should be thankful we're here," Ivy said as I walked up. "We never just say how thankful we are that it's a beautiful day, or that life is beautiful."

"Are you going to order alcohol?" I asked her. I was ready to tell her about the boy in the field, about what had happened. I wanted to now, to remove myself from everything here.

"It's my sister," Ivy said to a tall soldier on a bar stool.

"Hi, sister," the tall man said to me.

"I want two rum and cokes," Ivy said to the bartender and I sat down on the stool, next to the tall soldier with sun-dark skin who had a rip in his green beret.

Ivy pulled at her dress. "I don't like women," she said to me. "My friends are always male." She hadn't lit her cigarette yet. It dangled out the left corner of her mouth. From her satchel, she took out a box of the long kitchen matches Savta kept in the pantry in the house.

I turned from the tall soldier on the stool and saw my mother wiggling and dancing under a watercolor portrait picture of Lord Balfour, strung on the bone wall.

"This hotel was bombed by the Jewish underground in the old Israel," the tall soldier asserted his presence. "Did you know this, yaldahs?" He lifted up a drink that had a paper green umbrella, and a cherry pitched onto the sides of its glass container.

I lost my bearings for a moment.

"Are you from Florida?" He continued cheerfully.

"No." I said.

The waiter was pressing a tall dark drink across the counter to me.

"From where are you?"

"From Katonah," Ivy answered for me.

"Is that from Florida?"

"Not really," Ivy said.

I picked up my drink and stuck my tongue into its black, icy center. A circle had formed on the dance floor, arms across shoulders, legs kicking in the air, the accordion player worked up into a sweat. I was looking for my mother's head, her orangey coiffure in the mass of hair and bodies. Her face was red and sweaty. A wildness had set in as drums and electric guitars joined in on a fast rift of "The Girl From Ipanema." There was a singer at a microphone. "Tall and dark and tanned and lovely . . ."

I went back to my drink, taking another sip. The rum began to shuffle my brain cells and an image of my father's ashes shaken inside their gold urn came into my mind. I wouldn't tell Ivy what happened, I thought. I couldn't tell Ivy.

"The Amish pick grains from the stalks in their own meadows." I heard her saying to another one of the soldiers. A wiry adolescent, in uniform but sporting a Beatle haircut. "They milk their own cows." She blew out, and the smoke made a mushroom in the air.

"Are you this Amish?" The tall soldier turned back to me. Now, he was alternating between Ivy and me, making his movements a kind of swivel dance on the bar stool, his hips, his uniformed legs, his booted feet supporting him as he adroitly switched, back and forth, and back, and forth. His curls were black as shoe polish under his beret.

"No," I said to him.

"*Ma yesh?*" The tall soldier was still leaning over me." You have to want *some-thing* . . ."

"Oh, she would give her heart gladly—" the adolescent soldier started singing along off-key. The bar light was on Ivy's back. The satchel that housed her packs of Chesterfields was still opened, and some of her make-up had spilled out across the bar like a department store display.

"I can't stand it here," Ivy said now at the bar. "If you want to know the truth I despise Israel."

"Yes?" When the tall soldier turned back to her, his knuckle made its way slowly down the length of her lean body. "Would you like to go to Tel Aviv then?" He asked her. "To disco?"

"Yeah," she said.

"Ivy," I whispered, "do you want me to get lost? Do you want me to leave?"

"No. Hang on, Liana," she said to me. "Drink something."

The rum coursed through my throat. My knees felt suddenly cool under my skirt, and the glint of the bar's stone floor made me think of the ice pond in Katonah.

"And don't say anything else to this bartender," Ivy added. "He will soon figure out you're underage."

I wanted to leave now, but there was no way to tell Ivy that either. Now even the accordion player was dragged into the dancing circle on the ballroom floor, a record player was doing Hebrew national songs, taking over from the bandstand, the sounds of bare feet stomped on the wooden floor.

My mother was dancing the hora. "Liana!" I heard her shout. "Liana! Come! What're you doing all the way over there?" She danced towards the bar, barefoot, her face crimson, and wild. Then she was singing up to me, her two unpeeled nylon stockings in her closed hands.

I went down to her.

"Why don't you dance? Is it so terrible to have fun? Liana, forget the past. Live to survive! And hold my stockings, will you?" She lifted up her arm and dangled her stockings teasingly, almost tauntingly, in front of my eyes. "I shall dance all night I think. I have not seen my friends since twenty years. Put my stockings in your pocket, Liana. I will only drop them as I am doing my hora."

"Good, Mom," I said.

"Good, what, Liana?" She thrust the still warm stockings into my fingers. "Oy, that's my daughter! Take these," she said. I could feel her sweat in the salty nylon. "You have been watching how well I dance? Here, Liana." From the evening purse straddled across her shoulder by thin beads, she took out some pink lira bills and slipped them under her stockings in my hands. "Buy you and your sister some more Coca-cola. Have some fun!" And then, she turned and went back to the dance floor, her colored hair glittering under the chandeliers.

"What's going on?" Ivy shouted from the bar.

I went back to my bar stool and drew my mother's stockings out of my pocket and holding them up, let them fall to the floor. "Look. Snowballs," I said.

"The Amish don't live in the reality we give them," Ivy turned to the tall soldier. The adolescent in uniform had left in the time I had been with my mother. "And we might have all had other lives, I don't mean anything hokey. I mean essences."

The soldier's grip on her had become full of strange aggression. Inside the baggy green fatigues he was wearing, it was impossible to miss his suddenly attentive manhood. I could not help staring.

Several more males congregated around Ivy and me.

"There is another reality," Ivy was saying to another soldier. She had become both rigid and excited." The Amish pray. The Amish do not use modern appliances. You may not believe this, but I brought pictures with me from America, and they're in my room at Metadulah Street."

The light from the bar lamp fell on the tall soldier's face, his pale skin, the purple shadows under his eyes. "Oy," he said to me now. "Your sister talks about these Amish. From Pennsylvania she said. Is that in Florida?"

"No, not at all," I picked up my drink and licked the sticky foam ringed around its rim from the Coca-cola. There was no more rum in it, but it still smelled sweet.

The tall soldier's hand picked itself off his knee, moving towards me. I braced. And in that second some of the modern lights in the ballroom flashed on, spraying the room like sudden gunfire. There was a shout.

The soldier's hands jerked away, began doing complicated things with his holster as more lights flicked on.

"What is the matter?" Ivy asked. "What happened?"

The microphones on the platform rang with a hollow static, and the chandeliers' stream of yellow light was reduced to pale, weak veins.

"*Beh-vaka-shah!*" An officer climbed to the platform and addressed the crowd. "Attention!" More of the fluorescence from the ceiling flicked on. "*Slehah!*" The officer at the microphone shouted to the crowd. "*Zoozy! Yallah!*"

"Goddamn," the tall soldier said. "Even we search these old Meshuganeem here."

"What's it about?" Ivy asked. "What is going on here?"

"They are only doing a search. They look through the bags," the tall soldier said. "Today in Israel if the army is not familiar with you, they must search to make sure there is not, how you say, an intruder. Some of these old people have come from abroad, like you."

More officers barked orders at the confused, dislocated group as the soldiers pulled up a long table from the corner.

"A search?" Ivy asked. The tall soldier laughed.

"I know the Captain," he said. "The short fellow. He was in my training unit." He pumped up a pack of cigarettes out of his shirt pocket and offered one to Ivy. "A-mish—" he teased, laughing. "Amish girl, take, take. Calm down."

"But why're they frisking people here?" Ivy shrilled. "Why would they suspect people like us?"

"It's not like that, *yaldah*," the other soldier said. "They check everyone. There is a diplomat's son missing. You have not heard on the radio?"

The officer jumped off the platform.

Lines had formed on each side of the long table and my mother had pushed herself up in the left one. Her face was red with anger, and she already had her purse open. She turned it upside down and whacked it twice on the bottom. Lipstick, money, keys, and crumpled kleenexes tumbled out.

I touched my sister's elbow. My mother was hoisting her coin purse to the soldier's nose, spreading the bills out like a bridge hand, spilling coins on the tabletop. "Ivy—" I said.

"Will you tell Mom?"

"Tell Mom what?"

"I have to go now. I have to get back early," I shot off the stool, quickly finding my balance. "I want to sleep. Please tell her for me." I steadied my eyes on the polished floor, walking slowly to the exit arch. My mother was still scrambling the contents of her bag across the table, refusing to put them back inside her purse. An officer was walking over to her, but then I didn't look anymore.

I soon came to the wrought iron gate at the entrance of my grand-mother's house. I reached into my skirt pocket to find some lira to pay. I felt some warm; wormy raisins Doda Esther had given me days ago. They had melted into pulp and stained my fingers and the crumpled five lira I pulled out.

"*Shalosh*. Three," the driver said when I gave him the bills. He shook the lira out, studying the black pieces of raisins under the moon-light. Then he gave me two bills back.

Inside the stone house the foyer, dining room, and salon were all dark. I felt my way up the marble stairway to the second floor, think-ing: the dawn would be the best time to leave.

Only the milk trucks from the nearby kibbutz would be on the street at dawn, and the peddlers pushing their carts of fruits and bagelahs. I could walk up a distance and enter the vast barbed-wired fields from another entrance, from behind another tenement, or house, where no one here would see me. I could take the early morning bus into Tel Aviv. Forget about William, the boy, everything. There was still a way to get to Paris if I wanted. But, I must be sure to be out of view before the morning patrols arrived, the fresh lines of assorted military reservists and police asking questions. I held on tightly to the banister, it wasn't a long time away, I thought.

I could take the small valise I saw the first day I was here in the bedroom closet upstairs. I put my fingers in my skirt's pocket and found the raisins there again. I was hungry, I thought. That's all.

I threw a handful of the raisins to the back of my throat, and they formed a sweet paste on my tongue as I chewed. I finished them, walking up the marble stairway but an excitement, a thrill was also in my stomach, as if a sphere of nerves had caught and tangled up the vibrations in the King David Hotel, holding them there in a ball of air I wanted to release, exhale.

When I reached the top of the marble stairway, I went down the hallway towards my aunt's and uncle's bedroom, listening for the sounds of sleeping. Their bedroom door was closed, and it was dark inside their room. I turned the key of the hallway bathroom, and, inside, turned on the large bright bulb over the sink. Only a small window facing the pine trees on the side of the house was there to let the shine out. My aunt and Uncle Yakov would not be able to see anyone was here so late at night.

I stood by the W.C. and looked out the opened window at the dark outlines of thin pine trees, the now dry shrubs, thinking about William.

Then I went to the sink and opened the bathroom cabinet to find some "wash and dri" toilettes my mother left for us. A silver flask of talcum powder with its cap off stood between the nut- colored perfumes that, even in their fancy bottles, were turgid like this rough country—sweet and wild and disarming, like honey and vinegar mixed together. The opened flask of talcum powder breathed its cloud of scents. It was old and engraved. My mother's or Doda Esther's. I couldn't decipher the Hebrew initials. I reached for it.

I imagined the women of the same ballroom from the 1930s with their bobbed alluring hair and long skirts. The women of before, British wives with arms like elephant trunks married to mustached officer husbands who went to the hunting clubs that were still around the old city avenues of Jerusalem. The stately King George Boulevard still had haunts of the former class bars, vestiges of the clubs where officers had smoked tobaccos and there were the remains of the ruckus-inciting drinking dens, places where the lower ranked soldiers drank their beers separately from the officers, down the street. Where had my mother and Doda Esther and my mother's brother went to party then, when the British were here? Now there were boys with Beatle haircut splashed with tonicy scrubs on their skin, in rock bands. In my imagining of a past I could not touch, but only watch rise from hints and pieces left behind, my mother was another woman once, more innocent, more hopeful, whose body was fragrant with the old perfumes which rose up from the ballroom curtains, and still clung to their fabric.

Then William's face kept coming back. It wanted to lift the loneliness out of the room, strike back at it and the whiteness, and remembering the thickness of his thighs and calves, I was aroused.

I put the flask back with the perfumes. Then I began to undress, feeling the unbearable, dry night wind from the opened bathroom window crawl up my legs. When they fell to the floor, I didn't bother to hang up my denim skirt or my shirt. I went to the sink and stared into the bathroom mirror; at the smudges my black eyebrow pencil had made under my eyes. Then, turning the faucet on over the sink, I watched a drizzle of water drops. They plopped down like tears, then the valves made a rusty noise and the water stopped, I felt heavy clanging in the pipes, the sound that had become familiar now, a heaving. There would be no water.

I shook my head, looked back inside the bathroom cabinet. There was an old, crusty make-up compact on one of the shelves, an oval brown plastic thing belonging to Doda Esther. Crouching and pulling down my underwear, putting it between my thighs, I flashed up a reflection of dark curly pubic hair, salmon-colored folds and buttons and flaps. I rubbed the sensitive strip and brink between them with my fingers, afraid, but thinking of William again.

I fantasized I was wandering out in the streets beyond the border warning signs.

"Watch the street lights! Watch out!" William was calling me, his face stern, his eyes intense.

He grabbed me. I fell bare onto a bank of strong, ruling flesh, I was over his knee, and his lap was butter-soft as the fields. William was spanking me.

"You will only get hurt out here," He said.

I pretended my fingers were waifs in a storm as the waves began, pretended they had to take refuge within me as I pushed them deeper into the hole that was there.

I expelled out a vast pleasure. Then I stopped rubbing myself and stared at the redness that made my flesh there look raw as a sore gland, and the pleasure's finish came again without my own will. I looked up, out the window. The sky and the night wanted no part of this, I thought. And then, I felt a snap, a fierce, wet breath in my flesh. I turned back and stroked the tiny ruffle again, building up the waves. William. The waves rolled and built and crowned.

They were hot like death, these orgasms. They gave off a moan like mattress springs and a smell like curdled milk. When the palpitations and their finishes became weaker, I ground my buttocks with my fingers to make more of them. My compact mirror slipped to the bathroom floor, shattering.

My fingers returned between my thighs, encircling and testing the warm violence of the fifth or sixth burst. I stretched my neck, listening to what answer my body would give to the fear I would fall apart. I shielded myself with my arms, wrapping them around my shoulders. I bowed my head and picked up a shard of the broken compact, looking into it. I studied the scarlet ruffles, the fleshy tip that looked like a tiny cliff under the reflecting glass of the compact's shard as if it were opera glasses and I, at the theater. I tried to listen to what was happening inside me, to the emanations. I stood up straight, seethed in my own rushing flesh.

Feelings racketed through my brain. A pink dust had scattered from the cracked block of powder that fell as the compact shattered, and on the bathroom tiles there were smears and tiny clumps. I cleaned up the compact's dust from the floor with my hand, scooping and brushing it up and watching my skin turn red-pink as if it had brushed into a sugary strawberry cake mix.

In a light made up of swept shatter, dust, and the sweet syrup of the anemones, I was the toucher of fragile borders and brinks now. Part of what lay beyond the false hedges and gardens and the loud laughter of women who once knew better secrets about love.

I stood and looked again out the bathroom window. The breezes coming from outside through the window had begun to smell like moist herbs and were minty. Why was I crying?

With a bath towel hung on the rim of the sink, I tried to brush off my hands and put my skirt back on, I stuffed the broken compact into one of the pockets.

The glitter of the tiles on the bathroom floor began to sting my eyes, and I felt sick. Either the excitement or just the rum and coke I had drunk was coming up, and I rushed to the toilet and puked. The first noxious taste of vomit stung my mouth and throat. I pulled the long metal chain over the hole and watched my vomit swirl in brown rivers, but it would not vanish downwards. The toilet had no water to flush.

"Fuckface." Why did I do it, feel my inside like that? I whispered to the swollen face I saw in the mirror over the sink. "Fucking a-hole." Why didn't I go to the police station and report the killing? I knew where the missing diplomat's son was. I knew everything. Didn't I?

I went back to the toilet and stared into the hole. I cried, kneeling down, hearing the toilet pipes creak. I pulled the long chain down harder, but the spent water only bubbled. I remembered when my father had punished me, the one and only time. He took me by the shoulder and rolled me in his hands, I was a prisoner of both his anger and attention, a soft smack came from his hand like a lick from the wind. What had I done? I remembered now. I had run from his protection into the streets. There were cars.

I let my finger run along the lever of the sink's faucet. I took another look at my puffy face. And then, I took a slip of toilet paper and wiped it.

I ran my tongue along the edges of my teeth, curved it back, stroked the ridged palate of the inside of my mouth with it to feel if William's imagined kiss was still there.

I would get into my nightgown in the bedroom and watch the moon spool over the distant pine forest. Maybe I would write a poem, I thought, about eyes.

When I entered the stone bedroom, I closed the bedroom door and there was no light but that which came from the opened sliding glass doors of the upstairs verandah.

I tried to imagine the empty bus station at dawn; I tried to think the pleasure in the bathroom was not still with me. But, when I took the small valise from the closet and opened it on the cot, I already knew I wasn't going to the bus station, Tel Aviv or Paris. Slowly, I put my journal with the maps and extra underwear inside it, two changes of clothes, and other things I thought I would need for a long trip.

The Arabic dress my mother had bought me in the old city was still in the closet—billowy and black as the night. But, I closed the closet, and then I looked out the glass porch doors.

When I finished packing what I needed, I pushed the suitcase under the cot, to make it ready to pull out by dawn, after my mother, and sister came and they had already seen me sleeping. No one could suspect then anything was wrong, or going to happen.

By my bed near the glass doors, I took off my skirt and shirt once more, putting on my nightgown and getting under the sheets with my journal and Shaefer pen. I again tried to tell myself not to go back into the forest. But the soft, nameless face of the slain boy came again begging for my eyes.

I put down the pen and the journal. I sat up, awake to all that had happened since my father left. And when I looked out the window over the verandah, looked for the path which had led me up through to the pine forest, and the distant walnut trees.

William would be waiting for me, I thought.

I breathed out a raspy heave of air and excitement. I thought I felt the sweat of mother in the palm of my hand, the wet stockings I had held for a moment at the dance.

But, I whispered: "I'm somebody now, too."

At three a.m., my writing journal jabbed my ribs, my pen had fallen to the floor, I had dozed off. I heard the outside gates slam and the loud opening of the downstairs door.

"Oh-oh," I heard my mother say. She was coughing, as if she had caught a bad cold. She was alone. I didn't hear my sister come in the door.

I got up and out of bed. My mother slammed around some more before she went into the salon. I heard the sliding doors of the salon creak on their runners.

It was time to leave. I wanted to be gone before morning, before my mother went looking for me.

I remembered the other things in my small valise, my black eyebrow pencil, some novels, my passport, Sally Noakes' rabbit tail that she had given me before I left Katonah (it was in one of the pockets of a pair of bluejeans), a bag of raisins to eat on the way, soap, and tooth powder. The Arabic dress had felt heavy in my hands, but I took it off the hanger. I put it in with my clothes, thinking of the faraway old city, the gold-domes and their strange glint in the distances.

Now I listened to hear my mother come up the stairs. But no sounds came.

I tossed my nightgown on the cot and quickly pulled new underwear on, a fresh denim skirt, a short-sleeved pullover, and sandals. I held on tightly to the banister in the dark, my bag of belongings hanging by the valise's plastic handle on one of my wrists. Slowly, I went down the yellow marble stairway.

The foyer was still dark, cloaked at the end of the stairway in gray and black.

My grandmother's make-up in a china bowl under the foyer's mirror glistened as the moonlight came through the square glass windows of the front door and from the slit underneath. There was a stiff-backed chair near the mirror and the small table. If I were going to be with William and change my plans about leaving for Paris, I thought, it would be good to put some make-up on to look older. I put the small valise down, pushing it into a dark corner of the foyer. Then I went back and stood in front of the mirror and started putting some of the rouge and lipstick on. It was dark but if I leaned towards the glass there was a glittering like tiny white flames.

Leaning down to pick up a stick of eye shadow in the bowl, my elbow brushed against the table and the telephone fell to the stone floor; the receiver thrown across the marble. There was a loud bleat, like a military beeper, then the black receiver started buzzing. I leaped for it, grabbing the receiver, muffling its noise with my hand.

"Liana?" The salon doors opened, and my mother came running out. There was little light, but her nightgown was sheer, and I saw her white body underneath it.

"Jesus," I said. I stood and put the receiver back on the hook. I pulled at my skirt.

"What was that, Liana?"

"I dropped the phone."

"You are calling someone at this hour?"

"No, no."

"What' re you doing, Liana?"

"I don't know."

"Why're your clothes on? You haven't undressed for bed, yet?" My mother looked at my grandmother's make-up, opened on the table with the telephone book. "It's Savta's," she said to me, coming closer.

"I know it's Savta's. I didn't do anything to it. I'll put it all back. Look if you want." I hurried back to the china bowl on the table, arranging the make-up assortment.

"You'll put it back?" For that moment, her face looked like the interrogators at the King David, the officers who spoke with brutal voices.

"What were you doing with it in the first place, Liana? Tell me."

"Nothing."

"Don't lie to me." Her hands reached for my hair, and she yanked my face to her. The other hand slapped my cheek, the burn sending a shock through my head. " You've got to be kidding," she said. Then she swung again, pulling at my hair, but she missed. It went black in my head, and I said: "I hate you."

Already, my mother was shaking, pulling at her unbrushed hair remorsefully. "Liana. You know I didn't mean to hurt you." She licked at her lips and then, exhausting herself with these nervous motions, looked at me, imploringly.

I rubbed at my cheek with the flat of my hand.

Then she came up behind me and put her hands on my shoulders. "I am sorry, please."

I turned away from her, putting my fingers into the make-up bowl under the mirror, relieved she had believed I was just trying on the makeup by the mirror. I picked up a stick of Savta's lipstick and then let it drop back into the china bowl, making a clink.

My mother turned me around, to her. With her hand, she placed my burning cheek against her breast, she grabbed tightly to my head, she ran her other hand over my hair, holding me close to her sweat-moist body. "We will sit on the couch, in the salon for a few minutes," she said. "I am just upset. You must forgive your Mommy." She was yawning now. She went to the sliding glass doors of the salon and pulled them further apart. "Well, I'm sorry you left the ballroom early, darling," she said. " You could see how all of us in the Haganah are close. We don't even have to say a word. But, the dancing made me tired."

I went to where she stood in the room. On the musty stone floor was a long silky couch and, in the distance, a fireplace made of ivory. The salon was next to the downstairs porch, and the curtains had been drawn open so that the moonlight peered in.

It was steamy inside the room, and I smelled the almond bath oil and sweet, hot odor of my mother's flesh. The salon was lit by a copper-stemmed lamp, even the glow was sultry.

I coughed. She was making me drowsy. She was unbothered, non-plussed, had suspected nothing after all except that I would get into my grandmother's makeup. All the secrets of my being now amounted to no more than a whisper of effects. I jostled myself to bring myself back from her seduction, thinking how I had undressed myself and stared with a hand mirror at the layered, animal-like flaps inside me, pink and red as one would imagine a skinned body part—shocking and open—seeking out my tiny moon. In a few hours, the sky will be bright with morning, I thought, and I'll be on the road. As soon as she falls asleep, I will figure out how to get the valise from the foyer.

A photograph of Elizar was on the mantle over the fireplace.

"It gets so cold at night here," my mother said. "It is this terrible weather; it never knows what it is. It changes all the time from one extreme to another. It makes everyone not themselves."

"Where's Ivy?" I asked, resisting the light-full pull of the room, my mother. "Why didn't she come back with you?"

"She will be back soon. She stopped maybe to get her cigarettes." I looked away from her, into the night-darkened furniture. "Liana, what time is it?" She asked.

"Some time at night still," I said.

"Good, darling."

My mother went over to the armchair by the fireplace. From its seat, she lifted up a gray woolen blanket that had been neatly folded and held it up, its bottom hitting the floor. She looked at me, and her eyes widened. "This is just like the blanket my brother Elizar and I used to sleep under. I remember 'til now, the wool of the blanket on our skin, it was from Beit Karem. He was so sensitive, Elizar. He had eyes like yours. But, I have told you this."

It felt dangerous in the darkness with my mother all of a sudden. Her stories were always like part of a bad dream I was having— moving in the air like an odor.

"We will stay here by the photograph of my brother. You'll forgive your Mommy. I am very sick sometimes. And I am sorry I slapped you. Pain makes you love people more though, doesn't it?"

"I forgive you," I said.

She turned off the only lamp in the room. She walked over to the couch and touched the two thick, round cushions against its back with her stocky fingers. She picked the cushions up and dumped them on the carpet. "Liana, I think I can feel Elizar and he is trying to tell me to stay at Metaduleh Street once and for all. We can both sleep here tonight. You see there is room. I will lie down and put the blanket over us, and you can lie down next to me, under my arm." She stretched out, the army blanket in her hand. Her feet did not reach the end of the couch.

"I'm cold," I said.

Her arm went up, and she said: "Right here, Liana."

"I'm coming, Mom," I said. A raw tickle was in my throat. My mother's scents hung over us—foreign, gritty, inviting—the dirty nylons and slip she had worn to the King David—barely rinsed—lay flat on the carpet with the bra she had removed. Without taking off my skirt, I unbuckled my sandals. I lay down on the couch with her, lay by her side as she threw the blanket up.

Being close to her again, I felt good—she had always known how to make me love what repelled me, the smells of her body, their warm flow through the air like spices penetrating my pores before the lapse into inner chaos that sucked up the sensations of what would have been, in any other kind of relationship, one of nature's orgasms falling all around us and inside. It was so dark in the room I thought I was in a dream of night. I pulled at the blanket and stared into the approaching black excitement of being nothing at all.

"It's hard to sleep upstairs," she said. "The wind is too loud there." She had been like a good lover, my mother, I thought. She was both brave and foolish. She had loved kissing me as much as slapping me, and if I had wanted to remain in the house of her body, among its summoning creases, I would be warm and dozy now. I would be waiting with a flicker of interest in her new story, another one about loss, and self-sufficiency. She would feel that she was still protecting me against worse darknesses: my father's abandonment and the numbness I still felt whenever I thought of him.

Under the blanket she pulled at her nightgown, tugged at the large underwear she had on, her breasts loose and jiggling.

I looked at the picture of her brother Elizar on the mantle. Elizar's face was thin in the photograph, solemn, his eyes were foggy large ovals. It was true that I looked like him.

"I hope you weren't staying awake because you were thinking of your father," my mother said.

"No. I wasn't staying awake. I was winding down from that party. It was too much."

"Too much?" She looked down at me near her arm. She pressed herself against my side. She held me close to her and I was her comfort, but she was no longer mine." Too much?" She repeated.

I looked at her arm above my eyes now. Should I leave a note? I wondered. What should it say?

"That's another picture of your brother on the mantle," I said.

"Yes," she said." It was always so scary when we were children. But under the blanket it was warm. I slept so close to him."

She took my hand, lifting it up over the blanket. She spread out my fingers, staring down into my palm. "Savta said she can read hands. But you know. When you were born, I swore it was the happiest day of my life."

I opened my eyes to stay awake, to make sure I stayed alert and would not let my resistance fail. I turned my head to see the foyer through the glass doors, the black telephone and its table, but I could only discern distorted shapes. I could fade once more into my mother's bigger life, her always-larger story, before the dawn came. Why not as I had before, vanish into her? I already knew the drill. Something would excite me to her: dread, fear.

The Jerusalem night was cold and with the white marble floor and marble fireplace, the salon was freezing. Outside a window, I could see the porch and a clothesline. I heard the rustle of the stray cats and the night winds. I remembered wearing my father's bathrobe when it got cold in America—the long, blue one he left in the bedroom on his desk chair the same night he left us. There, surrounded by notebooks and novels I never would understand, lifted from his study, I had thought quite suddenly, perhaps I can be him—I am him. Whenever I appeared in my mother's bedroom, her face would brighten. Two years dead, would my father think that I had enjoyed taking his place beside her?

My mother let go of my hand. I counted the minutes it might take for her arm to fall off my bosom now as my eyes went around the room to the old carpet on the marble floor, the pictures of the lost brother and the antique clock on the mantle.

"This was the best thing I did," my mother sighed, "bringing you to Israel." She petted my shoulder, and there was the smell of roasted watermelon seeds and baked salt on her breath, the sweet immediate fragrance of skin as she petted my hair.

Then my mother's arm lifted off my chest, and I could see the girlish crook in her elbow. "Don't you see I have what I want? I'm with my family again." She began scratching herself, as if she had suddenly contracted a rash from the wool in the blanket. "And these people at the hotel would have loved you if you had given them a chance. After all, you're my daughter and I was very popular in those days you know."

The room smelled of dust. Against the power of my mother's invisible magnetic field, the air pulled at me like the outside winds to draw me back, I lay still. On the mantle, the antique clock clicked off another minute with its golden arm. Where would I leave the note? What should it say?

"I told you the story of Elizar when we went to the old city, you remember?" My mother asked, but she wasn't talking to me anymore. She was looking at her toes which had popped up at the blanket's end." I haven't thought of him in years, Liana. Not until this ceremony was to happen. Did I tell you?

I didn't answer.

She pushed at my thigh with her hip and drew on the blanket, but I wouldn't give in, I told myself. I couldn't give in this time. She would not be able to keep me there. No matter what new story she told. I stayed very still.

"Did you see how all the people rushed to dance with your Mommy? And I hadn't seen them for twenty years. The little man with the big nose was in the Haganah with me. He lives where I used to train, near Ramat Rachel, where I used to train for the underground. Did I show you the pictures of me and all the soldiers? Your mother. Tomorrow let's go get some French fries. I like where they sell them at Jaffa Gate. You will stay with me, won't you, Liana?"

I nodded, but I kept my eyes on the clock.

"La . . . deda-da . . . My mother began singing. "*Jerusaliem . . . hatikvah . . .* "

What explanation would a note give her?

My mother cupped her hands under one side of her face and, at last, turned the other direction from me. By the clock on the mantle, it was five a.m. when she started mumbling, the blanket dropping back over us. The moaning of the cats grew loud outside.

I got out from under the blanket without waking her. Then, before I knew it, I had picked up the valise of my things in the foyer, was opening the sliding glass doors of the salon.

I told myself if my mother came out that is what I would tell her, that the cats were moaning and look, I would say, I was about to go out to them, I'll be back, as soon as I quiet them with some bread, or a cracker left in the milk bowl by the garden steps.

But, she didn't come to bring me back this time. I made it outside, not onto the kitchen verandah but to the street where beyond me was a better entrance into the pine forest and vast field.

I could feel every muscle in the back of my neck as I left her.

The sun flamed over the terraced hillocks towards the West Bank. The night's mysterious cold had begun to die away. The miracle of warm air, open road was right in front of me. I tapped at my watch. It was five-thirty a.m.

I pulled up the small valise. I wanted to enter the back fields through the courtyard of another stone house on Metadulah Street. Then I wouldn't be seen from a window at my grandmother's house, maybe by Doda Esther, or maybe by Ivy if she had returned by then. That way I could meet up with the same path that ran behind my grandmother's house, go back to the pine and walnut tree forest and then to the spot where the boy was killed. Find William. The place we had been together.

A dawn barricade of sandbags and chicken wire was in the center of the uphill street going towards the new city. I strode quickly up the sidewalk to push my shadow into the long stretch of billboard movie posters along the way, thick photographs that looked as if they had been made of watercolors. I hoped my body would join the imaginary fairyland of American images. the Israelis saw but did not penetrate with their rawer reality. I wanted to become as unreachable as the movie screen. I brought my bag up to my elbow, hastened my stride, felt the early morning heat. The scents of the eucalyptus trees and goat's milk from the early vendors wheeling in their carts from Jaffa Road were dense in the air.

A few soldiers, some in jeeps, some on foot with their machine guns slung over their loose brown shirts, their morning beards on their chins, stood under the bus shelter. I could see that the military police had set up one of their sandbagged mobile posts further towards King George Boulevard, white lights were flashing on stanchions and there were border troopers inside stalls. Some of the soldiers in loose formations along the street were looking through binoculars at the West Bank hills. Mobile posts went all the way up the street to where I couldn't see, all the way to the plazas of the new city, and its modern buildings.

But, the houses on Metaduleh Street house were still shuttered. I trekked up the street, searching for an opened gate and courtyard. The dawn's yellow sun forced itself upon me, already the heat was intensifying. By Mr. Haggittee's tiny grocery shop, a crate of oranges lay squashed outside, their insides flat as the stone. Yesterday's rain had beaten what was left of their rinds and pulp and for a second, I thought they were a flock of birds, all fallen together to their death in the rain and drowned. The wrought iron gates of the still-sleeping houses and the real birds I saw now streaming down from the far away hills to sit in the dawn sunshine reminded me that there was another world I could pass into, far from the mobile military guard collected with the semblance of William's face painted photographically on billboard posters, the new demands of another Jerusalem morning and its political anguish.

I walked down the road. I reached the unlocked gate of a deserted courtyard behind one of the old houses and walked in.

The morning was deep and bright. And everywhere a sweet unseasonable tamarisk hung in the air. I did not know why I wanted to touch myself. But, it was my country this body, I thought. The only power I will ever have. It felt like heaven except for a tiny sadness that circled outside me in the wind and entered, gently, under my skin.

I hoisted myself over a stonewall fence at the end of the courtyard. I climbed, onto a way that would lead me to the back of my grandmother's house through the back fields. I heard the squawking of birds, a fluttering group of feathered refugees, white and blue, pecking at the berryless shrubs.

The rising globe of sun was above my head and I heard some choppers. Two yellow helicopters peeled away towards the Jordan Valley, towards the faraway rifts which scrolled up to the clouds, the cypresses, and ruined Arabic houses beyond the rolls of corroded barbed wire, still so distant The ground all around was raw light and yellow grass. Soon, the street, the whole scene of police and stanchions was below me.

I hiked behind all the houses of Metadulah Street, through the raw fields where no one could spot me, and then, reaching the back of my grandmother's house, I found the path again, towards the forest. This was where I'd hoped that William would be waiting. I couldn't remember where the clearing was where the boy had fallen, the spot of the

Outside me now, William still came. A thick trickle kept coiling, oozing from my spread legs.

Quickly, William pulled up his jeans, zipped them. He stood and lighted a cigarette.

"Twenty-five billion years ago, the Great Rift separated all the continents of the world," William told me when he awoke hours later in the morning. He rolled up his duffel bag, and I washed myself with some of the water from his canteen. He put his rain boots back on. Then he read to me from a book taken from his duffel bag. "The seas and oceans were created for all the countries, but here, look, the continents never separated. The deepest scar on the earth, this trough which is only rocks and hills. The mountains of Jordan and Israel are like Siamese Twins," he read, "moving apart at the rate of one centimeter and a half a year."

I looked out into the distorting waves of light and heat, flat-topped mountains, rocky cliffs.

"The swollen pair strives forever to finally separate and cannot perceive each other across the poor Divide," he read.

He had ball-point smudges on his forehead I saw, and his speech was a little like stammering but what he read was good. I let him forget we had lain next to each, touched one another, and more. He was like one of the boys from the junior high school cafeteria with the odor of macaroni and cheese on his breath with his "The History of Jericho", "The Caves of the Forgotten Apostles", and a biological treatise on the wild flowers of the Bible—like the ones on the terraced ledges of the hills.

From here, the Moab mountains shone like polished copper, the Jordan mountains stained the deep gray water of the wadis.

By nightfall, we opened two more cans of beans, and put margarine inside. The fatty margarine tasted good and it filled us. I knew from the first there was a chance to become something larger than a fourteen-year-old who had just run away from her mother, left behind in the house on

Metadulah Street. William handed me a book called: The Birdman Of Alcatraz." Have you read it?" He asked. I told him, no.

There were hundreds of varieties of the migrating birds here, he explained. The Great Rift Valley was a twenty-mile rocket shoot down from the distant hilltops. The deep trough he spoke of. In fact, herons, egrets, wrens, blackbirds, sparrows, goldfinch came up from there, and the famous black storks who were rarer than the white storks and more secretive. They were unusual, he said, these black storks. They couldn't survive in urban areas like the white storks and all the other birds. When the forests and the fields of their homes became too disturbed, the black storks searched for concealed places within the same region to make their nests and propagate their progeny. He had taken some good pictures of them, he said, the black storks. They were exceptional birds.

Before my eyes were pictures of birds and palaces, the great River Jordan and Valley, the world he described. Then the man and his steam went to sleep on the blanket.

If only for a moment my father could feel what I do sitting here, I thought, perhaps he would have felt different.

4

TWO WEEKS LATER, I awoke from a siesta nap. I watched the light crawl in through the window, and the shadows altering on the dirty, mouse-colored basement walls.

I stretched, my arms and neck were numb from sleeping. I was dressed in a muslin gown with long sleeves, its fabric as thin as paper. I looked out the window. The courtyard and garden were empty. The air was silent, but for the lashing of the summer wind against our makeshift cardboard window shutters.

William and I had settled down to live inside the cellar of a monastery we spotted the first night we crossed over the border. The abandoned building was somewhere between the end of the last Israeli military zone, five kilometers south of here, and the mountainous ledge overlooking the Jordan River, ten kilometers north.

The first day we were here, William had sent his parents a Western Union telegram telling them he was all right. That hot day, he drew out some old linseed oil from his supplies, and propped some loose boards up against a far wall in our cellar. "I want to see whether I can build a kayak," he said. "Take it down to the river bank. Soon maybe."

He had constructed a design, then he began sawing the boards. A Bedouin trader at a camp by a cemetery had ordered special epoxy for him, sandpaper from Amman.

What was my design? Did I have one? It was enough for me these bright days to have the reflections I saw of myself as a female on the window glass here in the monastery, the shadows William and I made together on our walls.

The monastery was built of sun-seared limestone blocks. A water tank stood outside the entrance gates, the tank's rust and emptiness giving the walled garden inside the complex a disreputable feeling. The garden was filled with shreds of litter, errant vines. The dilapidated chapel above our heads might have been the hideaway of a gang of thieves, with its cloistered vaults, and grottoes.

Here in this spot, I thought, there must have been a Village of Lepers, too. Long ago maybe. Sometimes I believed I could smell the mold of a thousand years in these cellar walls.

The first headline in the Israeli papers had appeared this Monday. William bartered with a Palestinian merchant to bring us some Jerusalem Posts when the man went furtively across the borders to sell his farm goods. "American Girl Suspected Killed By Jordanian Sniper," the first headline read. Could I have let this go this far? I took in the must of the evening. Into two weeks? Of everyone really believing I was dead?

The air smelled like goats and sour plums. In the early evenings here, the lizards that skated through the bushes looked almost translucent. We had hiked four miles into the Jordanian territory to find a place to camp. A decrepit sign had been left in the jasmine garden of the deserted monastery that appeared to us the first night of our sojourn. The sign read: "WARNING: YOU HAVE LEFT ISRAEL."

I shifted on the mattress and squinted at the thick-stemmed field oleanders William had picked for me, returning last night from the orchards. Placed in a glass jar on the top of a wobbly table made of bamboo and twine in the center of the room, the oleanders were my "anniversary" gift, he said, commemorating our second week together.

The petals of the wild flowers had felt as warm as blood flowing when I held them in my hand last night and thanked him. I wanted to be the one to put them in the jar. But, somehow I had never gotten up, out of our muslin sheets after lying with him.

Now I saw he had cut the stems, run his large hands over them, removing thorns and dirt, and put them in the jar himself. Where had he gotten the water? It looked so pure.

On a wobbly table lay William's maps and his personal things: recent letters from his parents, journal entries in a spiral notebook, photographs.

Thirty times a day in waking dreams I saw the slain boy catapult from a tree branch into the dust. In the blinding white sky of afternoons here, reality could be swallowed. Death had become part of a glittery quarry of inner thoughts that mirrored the rocky reaches outside, the vast brink of limestone and white clay. My naps were long and deep, not like the ones at Metaduleh Street in my mother's bedroom. I had found a reason to escape her. A man with a repository of secrets had let me into his life. I had been made love to as a woman. Triumph took hold of me now as it had almost every day William and I had been in the cellar, and it made me feel a little faint, blending into the fantastical aura of stonescape and barren land. There were no rich and moist fragrances here or loud voices. The dry air and the whiteness colluded with the hills, a foil to my mother's land.

The refugee camps had steep paths and white-yellow fields that reeked of dung. Sounds of muezzin and their daily chants echoed from the shabby mosques. The mud brick huts and tents were peaceful, even joyful, with no electricity or telephones. Ovens inside them were fired by smoking eucalyptus branches, bath water was warmed by fire. Fires smoldered, and smoke rose at night and in the mornings.

And there was fighting far away now. Gunshots heard at midnight, by dawn the air was still and quiet.

The surrounding desert hills and mountains created a moonlike, unreal landscape of caves and caverns and parched-white earth. Syria was to the north, past the Allenby Bridge, and further east were Jordan's mountains and valley, paralleling our lime-terraced hills. The nearest Jordanian town was a good 15 miles away.

The Christian Arabs lived in Bethlehem which was not in Israel in 1963, but some of them stayed here where the border signs were, in UN refugee camps that used to be sheep farms, groves for produce. They were not from families which, like my mother's, owned businesses, held engineering degrees.

My mother's friends, forced from their homes by the last war, "The War of Independence," left behind their villas and summer resort houses and could, like the birds, migrate back to the cities. Friends of my mother's father, mirror images and virtual doubles of the Silberfelds, middle-class or upper middle-class colleagues, were now in Amman or Beirut where they wouldn't have to worry about the water or the snipers. But the farmers, mostly Bedouin, had stayed.

All around us, farm families lived and worked off the dusty, unyielding land in the run-down camps of mud brick huts, deserted villas, torn tents, with their stalls full of goats and cows, olive tree groves, orchards, and citrus nurseries. For the last few days, we saw a jeep from the nearest town, the Jordanian military guards, canvassing through the winding dirt roads, binoculars strapped over their shoulders. There were Mercedes-Benz sedans which occasionally rattled through the narrow lanes, and when we saw the shiny metallic gleam of them, William and I hid in our cellar and shuttered the windows.

One night (had it been a Sunday? It was so hard to keep track of the proper names of each day) I heard a helicopter, and I wondered if it was my mother in the plane searching the forest for her missing daughter. Several times, I had tried to walk back to the spot—where the barbed wire was before the gunshots sounded, to where, even if my mother had tried to cross through the long path in the pine forest—the metal spokes would have blocked her search further, and the snipers in the trees.

I stood, then lifted the muslin sheet and shook out the dust. These past few days, I was idle. My sketchings of the slain boy from the forest and my journal entries had stopped. William had decided that asking about the boy made us too suspicious. The military jeeps were coming more frequently into the UN camps.

This evening, I had promised to pick the tomatoes off the vines up the road and clean them for a supper salad.

I picked up our plastic AM/FM Admiral transistor radio from the floor and walked over to William's duffel bag and pulled out a box of batteries.

I jimmied the back of the transistor off, took out the dead batteries, plunking them into a can we used for garbage, and replaced them, flicking the radio on. An Arabic soccer game, somewhere in the playing fields of Beirut, blasted. Quickly, I flicked the volume down, and switched the channel. A woman with a British accent was talking about John, George, Paul, and Ringo being "currently in her record collection." I turned it up, then gathered up my journal and walked over to the window sill.

Placing the radio on the floor and trying to make myself comfortable on the sill with my journal, I studied the boards for William's kayak. Three were propped up against the far wall under some peeling pictures of saints. Four women carrying alms and rosaries in their white fingers.

A Paul Anka song shared the tinny static from the radio, and I shuddered thinking of my old life, the green-painted New England furniture in my bedroom, my sister's LPs on the ivory coffee table of our Westchester living room.

I remembered an abandoned clapboard house Sally Noakes, and I had spotted on a walk on the train tracks in Katonah leading into Manhattan. The house had stood cadaverous against Westchester's sky, up on a hill, with peeling shingles, standing alone. House flies flew around it in bouquets of gray haze. Its burnt grass yard looked muddy in the dusk light. A rusted fence collapsed around it, and its face was splintered, as if an explosion had taken place nearby.

Sally and I had climbed the hill and snuck in through a busted window. The walls were scratched and bare.

"Wait for me to get back with some food and we'll explore," she had said.

I had watched her go.

On the moldy planks I sank down on my stomach, my face pressed into the floor. Then lay aroused by a smell like shoe polish and fall leaves. What did I really want? I had wondered. My desire always meant pleasing someone else. I wondered what was real desire anyway? It would come to me in a cool, dark room like this, aroused by a man's body like the one in the Rodin sculpture I saw on a postcard once, I told myself.

Now it is when I have love, I thought, remembering that day with Sally.

I had believed that day, too, that love would come to me in a room of scraps, austere, maybe an abandoned building, like our monastery.

I pulled out a letter I began before I had drifted off for my nap this afternoon. It was tucked with all my letters inside my journal.

Dear Sally,
It may be that getting this letter astounds you but it to describe where I am."

There were other letters. Several of them.

Dear Sally,
In the beginning of the summer, around July, the American Charges D'Affaires's son ran away from Jerusalem . . . Guess where he is? If you get this letter, don't tell anyone . . . Finally Liana is in love. I wish I could tell you all about it . . .

I never finished my letters. There were folders of them, also poems, loose-leaf papers, underlined Arabic words to memorize. One unfinished to my mother explaining where I was, and not to believe I was dead. All unmailed.

I put them all back under the journal's cover. Then I breathed in the fresh air blowing in from the opened window and looked up at the peeling pictures of Saints on the cellar's walls. There was Saint Stephen and Saint Christopher opposite the four women with their rosaries and, I learned the second afternoon William and I lay on our mattress, a female saint named Lucia. She had matted black hair and watched us when we ate and slept. I learned all the names of the saints. The Saint Lucia on our wall was cold as a winter night in Chicago.

"The police have come to my shop—" a woman at a kiosk in the nearby camp had told me two days ago, "many policemen. From Jordan, *habibi*. Come to ask questions and show us photographs of you. Maybe someone call them from the other side where the Jews live. I won't say more words, *Sette*. Careful."

Near his duffel bag lay William's blueprints, a map down to Jericho with notations on some new caves rumored to have more fragments from First Corinthians. They kept turning up in some of the caves there, with other lost portions of the original apostles.

New and even more elaborate charts and diagrams were tacked on the wall behind his writing desk. The information in the Arab papers and on the Jerusalem radio station was controlled, but from the Arab version of "The Jerusalem Post" we could at least find out that border skirmishes were close by and how far the war over the Jordan water supply had advanced. The monastery was too near the barbed wire borders between the two armies for it to be safe for us to take the kayak through the fields, to the land's end in the bright sunlight. Israeli troops were camouflaged even here in Jordan and Muslim snipers were in the bushes. We could too easily be heard in the bushes, scraping the ground and, dressed in our new muslin clothes, mistaken by either side as the enemy. At least William and I had figured out the time of day the Israeli soldiers in their camouflage were least likely to be present.

In the nights, our radio played news about the hostilities between Jordan and the Syrian fighters who bombed water dams in the Golan and the Sea of Galilee to prevent the water from reaching Jerusalem. During the dinner hours and in the early morning, when Israelis on the other side were eating their breakfasts of tomatoes and cucumbers and yogurt, and hoping there might enough water in the tap for their tea and Nescafe, the news continued to report that no agreements had been reached between the Syrian and Lebanese fighters and the Jordanians here. The West Bank and its population of refugee farmers were caught inside the battle over what to do about Israel," the "water problem," the precious flowing streams. A Navy vessel had engine trouble out at sea somewhere near a coast in Maryland and, homesick one night William and I listened to reports of John Kennedy giving a "Profile in Courage" medal to the American seamen who brought the vessel safely back. The French had trained a mouse to travel into outer space, he wore a space suit with a corset and springs. At the same hour, an A-bomb had been tested in the Sahara. William and I kept switching the channels. The reception was bad, and the local Arabic songs and singers sounded like a swarm of bees.

I kept house these days, sweeping up the dust, scraping mildew off the windows, washing our clothes in basins with ammonia and lemon, and making our meals.

From the radio William had also learned that travel to Bethlehem, the Dead Sea, and the Jordan Valley was too dangerous for all foreign visitors until further notice from the Jordanian military guard. He listened for news about the archeological digs going on in the caves of Abu Dis. Some European academics had come into the area last week. William had already gone to their camp without me with his maps, and scrupulous notes.

He asked me to get up early in the mornings to watch the kayak when he took it outside a few times, into the garden to let the sun dry its epoxy and wet glaze. He left it propped up then—against a cypress tree like a curvy monument or trophy.

The farmers' boys were also up by dawn, and William didn't want anything to happen to the kayak.

It gave me an odd feeling standing there by the water tank, the summer sun on my hair, scaring away kids who, recognizing my American denim skirts, shouted out: "Hey, girlie," and then ran away.

The Bedouin farmers helped William and me pick tiny grapes off some vines by our water tank in the monastery's garden. The rough faced farmers with their keffiyehs and long poles had shown William how to fish for olives in the fertile trees by the road. They were strange and kind. One of the farmers had taught William how to search some of the white soil by his hut, comb the ground for fallen almonds and peel the succulent, oval nut with his front teeth the way they did, sucking out its sustenance and sweetness. The farmers spoke in low Arabic tones, laughing at his sunburn, his mass of accumulated bright brown freckles.

The farmers' boys wore white handkerchiefs on their heads, but their faces were raw from the kharmsin winds. The heat reached 102, dry, unrelenting, the shade under the cypress trees was as devastating.

The sound of some farm tractors out the window gave me a start. I looked down and studied my bare feet. The shrubs and stones these past days had cut into the skin of my bare toes and heels, and, drifting again into my thoughts about these two short weeks, I remembered the Arab vagrant boys picking car parts off abandoned vehicles on the sides of the road into Ramallah; using the worn car tires for soles to their sandals.

William and I spent afternoons in the fields, and sometimes some of the boys came to sit with us and tell us about flying saucers, how they saw one fall from the sky when it was midnight. You could see them sitting on big rocks, looking for flying saucers in the fields. The Jordanian children's books were filled with such stories.

Near old deserted villas, to the bridge that crossed into the old city of Jerusalem, the grapes were bigger, purple, and white. Their skins were sweet and the wagons full of farmers went out in the mornings to pick them and bring them back to the shops in the camps to sell to the UN workers and other Arabs who came down from the cities and towns. Stalls of fat and juicy grapes and wild tomatoes with whizzing wasps overhead had begun to proliferate in the center of the camps where there were cafes, too, and a few kiosks that sold the American newspapers, "Le Monde," and "The Jerusalem Post".

William found the relics of old Palestine by the orchards: mosaic tiles, gargoyles, and pewter once belonging to the gardens of the vacationing Sultans. They were buried in cacti and dry sandy ground, converted into decrepit farming tools that the Bedouin used, along with abandoned, debunked wagons and bits of British exploring gear from the open expeditions once possible down to Jericho and Eine es Sultan, before World War II came, and then the Israelis—the scrambling of boundaries and borders and rebellions. There had been days of sunshine and self-indulgences, campfires, and akar-drinking with the farmers and the Bedouin women. We held hookahs filled with hashish as pungent and delicious as the figs. The farmers seemed resolute, but random incidents around the orchards were daily now. Gunshots could be heard from tree tops, and strange Arabic youths appeared in the woods from the far-off cities, keffiyehs pulled all the way around their mouths so that only their eyes showed. They were dressed in military green and wore boots, not sandals.

Unemployment would soon be rampant in the camps, the crops, vines, and trees, depleted of produce by August.

The farmers were trying to get their picking completed before the winter came, maybe to move their families to safer camps down near Jericho. The orchards had already stopped producing oranges and tamarinds, all the farmland would soon be suffering. Well-dressed businessmen drove on the roads, their polished looks showing the boys and their father's glimpses of the cosmopolitan life in Amman, the commercial districts of Nablus and Ramallah full of factories and schools, apartment buildings, cafes, and restaurants. The heat waves had begun, and the trees were losing their leaves. The stalwart fig trees alone were bearing fruit as they had promised, like women in their last pregnancies—the ripe and sweet figs dropped into the landscape soon to be barren.

William went a few times into the orchards with the Bedouin, and brought us fresh food: fruit and bread, olives. The farmers paid him in groceries. The orchards were few, but in distances from the road you could see the patched tin, the water pumps and old tractors, women washing clothes in the wadis under the stoney mounds—white bumps of limestone like breasts protruding up from the dry grounds, some caverned, some terraced with more limestone and olive trees. William brought us some good fresh berries from the Christian Arabs who grew them, before we found out they used their own shit from the W.C. as fertilizer to grow the vines.

Yesterday, I had walked with William to the end of the monastery's entrance path and listened to him use the Arabic we learned at night. "How are you? How is your health? *Izzay el-sehha?*" He always used simple and familiar English expressions and then quickly followed them up with the appropriate translations into Arabic to make people think they could understand him easily, without any strain or confusion, to make people feel comfortable and not stupid, mixing both languages as easily as he could and making of them an easy broth. "Please go ahead," he would say, "Please come in. *Itfaddal.* Hello. Salaam. Peace be with you. *Salamu alayhum.*" From his booklet of Arabic in the evenings we read quietly in the cellar before bedtime, he mastered the basic Arabic salutations and sayings, the most traditional greetings." *Kattar kheirak,*" he would say to the Bedouin farmers and Palestinian shepherds. "May God increase your bounty."

The sun was going down outside now, containing a promise of a fine evening. The cellar walls were a disconsolate gray. I listened to the radio playing "If I Fell For You—" and I imagined vanishing forever.

After a while I went to our closet and threw one of my tee-shirts over my muslin dress. Pulling at it, its scratchy dried and matted threads, almost completely stiff from so many washings, I thought again about my mother. I saw her ambling up the long marble stairway at Metadulah Street to change into some dress and go to another celebration at the King David. I even wondered how long she had looked for me, if she believed I was dead.

My fingers went to feel my hair. The brown strands were flat from the water in the tank outside in the monastery's garden. But they smelled like figs. The Arabic shampoo we used, William and I, was the color of chocolate and thick as syrup.

I checked that the sheets on our bed had been carefully dusted and folded, remembering when William bought the mattress for our bed in one of camps.

"Now we are together in a different way than the night in the forest—" William had said to me that evening, and we were hugging and fanning each other in the dust and dark. With all of our clothes on.

Several minutes of silence passed, and I had turned on my side. "Do you think you'll be all right?" He asked.

"All right?"

"Are you too hot?"

He had been holding me, his foot touching mine, and his ankle rubbing against mine reassured me. His fingers felt underneath the rim of my panties, giving a hardy hug to my seat as if my bottom were a face and he were warming it, but he didn't touch me further. How strange it seemed. His caresses on the insides of my thighs that night brought me to pleasure as he talked. And his body was as attentive as if he were entering me. But, his member remained held in behind his zipper, as if in a cave. I had on my ragged denim skirt, my shirt with the bumble-bee on its breast pocket. He lay next to me, and he gave off a heavy breathing, he was heavy all over himself, he asked that we be quiet.

"I'm very sorry about—things," he had said after some minutes passed.

"What do you mean?" I said.

He had taken my hand and made his fingers tight around it, squeezing it as if it were a lemon. William's face took on the same look of remorse and self-accusation it had the night in the forest. As if, after a long and tortured anorexia, he had finally found a food he could devour only to discover the terrifying drive of his appetite, and the fragility of the object of his desire.

Darkness had fallen. We heard the last wagons of the farmers on the road, going to the Bedouin huts. I smelled his love. There was tension building in his testicles he could not release. His sadness left an almost tangible odor in the air, like burnt bread, but when I inched my body close to him, pressed against his side, he was better. Giving me instructions on how to do our chores again. "You're different about things," he had said.

"I'm different."

"No, that's not what I meant. I didn't mean different from everybody. I meant, you're different about things. Different than the other girls I was with."

"Then thank you."

"Well, thank you," he had answered.

When he had fallen asleep and, I was in his arms; the sheets were like sails. I imagined walls made of the Jerusalem oleanders and felt the arid land stirring like a basin. Whole mountains passed in my fantasies—fig trees, birds, and helicopters, otherworldly fragments competing as the solitary pleasure in my sex finished. Only twice did the smell of the bedroom at home in Westchester and my mother's stockings enter these spaces. William had moaned in his sleep, but his moans were grateful and blissful, too.

Now we slept with our clothes on every night.

He seemed to enjoy and be thankful for the simple pleasure of my lips on his, my hand on his, his fingers on discreet and select parts of my body. My heart beat too hard, but it pleaded with me to prolong the sweetness of his imprint in those shadows, the new experience of him brushing at my mouth. He could recreate me with his eyes, this stranger, while sirens howled in the distance outside most nights, more helicopters like yellow pelicans in the sky.

By the bamboo table where our oleanders stood in their jar, I picked up our latest Jerusalem Post from the floor now.

There hadn't been any more stories about William's disappearance. And after a few more articles about my death, we were all but forgotten by the reporters. "What Ever Happened To The Free World?" was the headline on the paper in my hand. Then there were photos of Charles de Gaulle in some garden in Paris; I turned the page to another article. I read: "'No one need tell us that the Communist menace isn't deadly serious,' Dean Rusk was quoted as saying this afternoon in response to the recent outbreak of violence in the Middle East."

My ID card was on the writing table. We were instructed to obtain and wear cards in Sheikh El-Dahr, the main Arab camp nearby because we were white and foreign. The Jordanian police had stopped us at an army post, and we were shuffled inside a stone police station, where it felt like a hundred flashbulbs popped around us, taking our photographs. Either the length of William's beard, or his extreme weight loss had thrown them off any scent that he might have been the missing diplomat's son. Or, the phone call to his parents had stopped the hunt. We don't know, but they didn't question us further.

A day later we returned to get our ID cards, with the tiny gray and white photographs on them.

I stared outward, assessing the outside temperature by the intensity of darkness cloaking the sky. Since the Arabic women in the shop had told me about the police coming into her shop, I had stayed close to the monastery these past two days. William went twice to the kiosk alone to get our groceries.

My ID card on the writing table read: "Dorian T. Karchimer." We had changed my name from Liana Bialik. What had the T. stood for? I forgot, and then, just as abruptly, remembered." Tree." We had given me the new middle name "Tree" when I changed the rest of my name.

I put down the Post and picked up a comb, pulling it through my hair, trying to make it grow faster while wondering if there would be enough water in our large bathing pan for me to splash on my face, on my sweat.

I stood still, gazing out the window. The evening was at its most beautiful in the monastery's garden. The sun was just setting, and it was quiet, the soft dark tinted with lavender.

Back at the pegged mirror, I still looked boyish, even in the muslin dress, except for a rounding that had begun to take place in my thighs and breasts. Drawing it out from my bosom, I put my fingers on the necklace William gave me the first Wednesday we were here, a wooden crucifix he bought in a kiosk. From touching it, the smell of sandalwood stayed on my fingers all day. I could tell none of the farmers I was Jewish.

I put the crucifix up under my eyes on its silver chain. Its dark wooden back gave off a faint scent like vanilla. I turned it over and stared at my fingers, holding this new world.

The news of my "death" had only been in the Jewish papers and since casualties on both sides were ill-reported, and miscalculated, it hadn't mattered much who I was, or if I was anybody at all. But for my mother who was the one, I was sure, who called the Jordanian police to come looking for me.

It felt as though I had been here a long time.

I studied the shadow I made against the white corners of the cellar's wall, and the atmosphere in the dark cellar lifted. "My name is Liana," I whispered.

We had spent just enough time in this cellar these days for me to get to know what William was escaping from. We found ourselves surrounded with pieces of our pasts and hopes. "So you didn't know about the "I Love Lucy Show?" I asked him again last night. I had in the course of these days learned that because William had lived in so many foreign countries, most of the television shows everyone else knew by heart weren't even familiar to him.

"What's it about again?" He asked.

We fell silent then, as if he had missed out on a religion. We settled for not mentioning his physical trouble, lying next to him, still fully clothed and his body wanting mine, but his responses forestalled by some other force within him, paralyzing him. He was working so hard on the back exercises he hoped he would solve it. My heart both rose and fell.

"My mother's eyes got bad in Chile," he told me outside in the garden back in July. "She lay in bed most of the time depressed when we were in South America. We got these Swanson frozen dinners. That's when my brother Carl tried to burn the school cafeteria down. My father made us believe that if we misbehaved in any of these foreign countries, we could cause World War Three. He has a mean streak, he gives us orders. *Can't you get it right?* He hollers at us. My mother is always pretending to be a helpless little girl. But, she is genuinely terrified of the world. It's a frightening, damaging place, her world. My brother and I have twenty first-aid kits between us. At least."

William's diary lay on top of a pile of laborious blueprints for the kayak. A few days ago, he had left his there, open. I didn't go near it, staring at his blue fountain pen that gleamed in the sunlight when the afternoons began here. Then, each day he left it open, more pages poured out by his steady and large hands. For the past two weeks, it had tempted me when he went to work.

Now the opened window was blowing at it, some of the loose white pages upturned. He had been working late last night, and his diary was open. I couldn't help it. I finally bent, unable to resist. I read:

"...*it isn't selfish at all,*" he had written.

When? I wondered.

"Because I don't know what I want of you. I deliver myself over to the unknown in coming to you. I am entirely without reserve or defenses, stripped entirely into the unknown."

What did he mean?

I picked up several more pages. There were diagrams of the lower back and hands, drawn at different angles with arrows pointing to the sketches which looked like insects or vertebrae.

"*Some tensions are universal,*" William dated this page: July 5, 1963.

"*. . . These tensions are reflected physically in the inhibitions of vital functions ('I'm scared of life, not sure I want to live it') These areas are: adrenals, anus, genitals, spinal nerve center.*
This calls for a specific program concentrating on the line of the pelvis, spine, neck, and head...exercises involving new and different stress, stretches and releases to discover old body patterns of tension and relaxation.

Exercises which relax sympathetic and non key muscles to facilitate approach to key and essential muscles.

Exercises which stretch and release key substitute muscles."

I had read enough.

The first week we were here, William had shown me the Life maga-zine article about his family, folded to a billfold photo size inside his diary. Sitting cross-legged now on the floor and readjusting the blanket over my shoulders, I unfolded it and read again about William Coons Sr., slowly taking in the figures whose imagined voices and forms had filled my dreams this siesta. The interview was in this May of 1963, when William had first disappeared. William's father was seated in an immaculately furnished living room somewhere in Jerusalem. In the photograph, Mr. Coons sat in a leather swivel chair he must have had exported to him from a Sears Roebuck in the States, his legs crossed, a white handkerchief folded neatly in his blazer. He was a lean man whose carrot-colored hair looked frosty in the black-and-white picture. He wore the kind of bifocals with plastic rims I had seen on my ele-mentary schoolteachers and had a posed face, which had turned to the picture-taking camera purposively.

Mrs. Coons was in a photograph on another page. A large, bovine woman with her hair in a ponytail and her hands groping. Her eyes were covered by sunglasses, and by her side was a seeing eye dog, a col-lie on a leather leash. I stared again into the unmistakable fact of her blindness. Mrs. Coons, seated on a folding chair on the veranda of some embassy house, was (it had taken me two or more seconds to realize when I first saw it), completely blind.

"Have the Coons Lost Their Eldest Son to the Terrorists? was the caption. "Will the Water Project Conflict Mean More Loss for This Family?"

I could see she was once pretty with large, innocent eyes, Mrs. Coons. She wore shiny earrings the size of plums and a necklace with stones as big as her eyes around her now thick neck. I bent down and read the black ink headlines, feeling the voices that made up the daily news and thinking of international journalists typing on old Reming-ton typewriters on the limestone porches of cafes, typing out, with all fervor, Ben Gurion's resignation in May, the flattening of Syrian road-blocks and dams where the water was supposed to run forever from the River Jordan into the new Jerusalem, and there, on the first page, as good as any other story of irresolvable conflict was the story of William. In the following pages of the Life article, William was in photos with his mother and father, wearing his L.L.Bean jeans, and plaid Brooks Brother shirt. Smiling. They must have been taken a year ago, his hair was long, and his face well-behaved, and vacant. But, what could I say about those parents?

In a second photograph of Mrs. Coons, her sunglasses were off and I could see her white tiny eyes that had balls without centers, without any sight tissues, just a blank.

" When did you contract the blindness, Mrs. Coons?" a reporter asked her in the magazine interview.

"We are happy to be here in the Middle East," Mr. Coons responded. "But to answer your question. That would be about three years ago in South America. We have to travel so darn much."

It was clear that the article had to be carefully edited. Another spread of shots showed the room in which his parents entertained Embassy guests with its mahogany and leather cocktail bar, martini shaker, and Planter's peanuts.

The article ended with a recipe for "Brunswick Stew" Mrs. Coons gave to the reporter.

I folded the article back into a neat billfold and slipped it behind the page in William's diary where he had made a list called: "How To Meet Girls" which read:

1. Dating services.
2. Maintain all contacts with everybody, make a friend out of everybody; they might just throw a party where I can meet a fine woman. Remember: even though I don't like the person I can meet people through him or her.
3. Join some kind of interest club—take classes, join clubs.

4. *Be more outgoing on the street, make remarks to strangers,*
strike up conversation. Waiting rooms are good places.
5. *Singles bars, sporting events, parties...*

Finally, I pulled off my muslin dress, slipping into clean clothes. At last
turning to go, I went back to our stack of freshly washed clothes,
pulling out my sneakers, and exchanging the muslin dress for my old
denim wrap-around.

I went over the shopping list William had left for me, things I was
to have kept memorized in my head besides the epoxy: black tooth
powder, fruit salt for laxatives, iodine, Witch Hazel.

I put on the sneakers, drew some lira out from our stash inside a tin
can, and ventured up the steps, leading out of the cellar.

The early evening was at its most beautiful in the garden. I came out of
the monastery's pathway into the glow of moonrise, and hiked to the
road where, turning, I suddenly saw, among the rocks and laurel on the
left shoulder, a shadow cast on the thicket by our phantom spy. She
glanced at me, nodding as if she could read my mind as if to say: *yes, I*
have been watching you. And then, mounting her English racer bicycle,
she pedaled down the road, not turning back again.

She bicycled to an untraveled bend in the road, the dying light
falling luminously on the back of her long black hair. Then she vanished down the stretch of dust and dirt as a rumbling came from a long
way off from the direction in which she traveled. Soon, a cart pulled by
goats with two shepherds behind it carrying whipping sticks emerged.

"*Yallah!*" The shepherds cried, hitting at the necks of their goats
with long lashes made of Cypress trees. The long day's work and sweat
glistened on the animal's tired backs.

The moon sailed in the sky, white as a sea cap. But, there were still
no stars.

The Arab procession kept coming up towards me. I saw now it was a funeral parade of red banners, men in blood-red cloaks carrying wooden poles and an opened casket over their shoulders. Racing behind the men with the coffin were three young boys carrying stones the size of coconuts in their fists and shouting: "*Falastine! Falastine!*" Palestine. Their heads had been shaved, and there were flies buzzing around their dirty noses and faces.

I moved to the side of the road. They must have come from the camp where William and I saw the Bedouin fishing for olives on the few old trees a week or so ago. I watched the procession disappear down the road to the Allenby Bridge where they made a spinning U-turn to the North, to Ramallah, and distant Amman. Then it was almost quiet.

Suddenly, the woman reappeared on her bicycle, wheeling quickly past the shepherds who were back on the road. Then, just as quickly, she disappeared in the other direction. And I was alone.

I stared down the raw dirt road, wondering if she had turned off at the bend, going on the deserted cacti-bordered road that stretched east there. I had never traversed that road, even in the daylight, with its overgrowth of wild vines. I had been told the villas there had been abandoned and that there was a cemetery there, holy to the few Muslim families inhabiting the refugee camps. Off-limits. Even the shepherds and their children and goats did not go beyond the spot on the road where an old sign announced what I assumed had been another resort town for wealthy city Arabs, standing in the same forbidden territory.

I looked around the darkness. Then I turned onto the prohibited route towards the villas and the cemetery. There was no light but that of the moon's, and soon I lost my bearings and all sense of direction. It was too late to pick tomatoes; I could barely see where the vines lay. The deeper part of evening had started, the stars inflamed in the sky. Stones gleamed under my sneakers, like shells on a beach, and soon I noticed a small rivulet. The soil beneath me grew wet, and I followed the line of water onto a footpath leading into the abandoned town. A sudden breeze from down below swept up, and I felt the thinning denim of my skirt.

I walked for twenty minutes on the path looking for the woman. Then there was no more trail. The rivulet stopped abruptly, drained imperceptibly into the dirt. My navigation through the empty place became treacherous, my shoelaces catching, my legs scratched by the shrubs.

The night expanded with stars that burned instead of sparkled. A dozen or so black herons flew low over my head, the wind carrying their cries further eastward. I kept walking, eventually coming to a set of rusty iron gates, tottering on their hinges. I pulled one opened. There, before me, was a cemetery. The Muslims had put up signs of warning in broken English and Arabic. "Not Permitted No Visitors" "Place Forbidding to Dogs." "Attention! Danger!" The tombstones flickered with the ghosts of the endless dead. They were covered with a powdery mildew the color and smell of boiled cabbage. Many were crooked and cut into teeth by the endless dry heat of the days here, and there were moths flitting around the crawling vines. The holy site was overgrown with prickly cacti, forlorn tamarisk.

I was trying to guess what time it was when, startled by the sound of leather sandals scraping in the dirt of the path, I heard, "Excuse me, you are American?"

It was the woman on the racing bicycle.

"Don't be scared, American girl," she said.

I stared into her copper-colored face, the bright eyes. She was dressed in a traditional Arabic gown that was stately at the same time it was skimpy. It was decorated with pharaonic figures. Around her shoulders she wore a lavender, chiffon-like keffiyeh. But it was torn. A thick leather satchel, like a camel bag lay strapped across one of her shoulders. It was filled, heavy with things.

"I have things to do here," she said, letting her shoulder bag slide off her big arm to the ground. "Important things. My name is Miri. I am friend of Ada. Your emah." The red hue of her lips was from being blistered, her lower lip had dried and cracked in half, discolored like a scar. She stepped a few inches away from where the shoulder bag had dropped, closer to me. "You have come here before? Syrians around here, much of them." I took two quick steps back and caught onto a tombstone to catch my balance. It was dark down among the grave-stones, a quiet dark.

The lavender moonlight that descended on me seemed darker than night. Miri kicked sharply at the dirt on the ground. "One Syrian put bomb inside dam. Don't want us to give Israelis water. The Syrians from the north. One week ago this happens."

"Was that the funeral we saw?"

"Not funeral. Children not dying here from dam and bomb. You know not what happens to them. I tell you. But another day." Her presence shifted abruptly from a strong, nearly masculine self-possession, to a warm, maternal tenderness. "You are a Jew, yes?" She asked me.

"I am."

"And you come here to this graveyard?"

"I do but—." I rubbed some of the dirt off the sole of my right sneaker, lifting my foot. "I stopped here, I can explain but— What' re you going to do to me?"

I felt as though I was sliding on some wild and unstable stream of air.

"Do to you?" She started laughing.

"I don't know you. "I let my foot slip back down. On one of the flat-topped graves, I saw faint drops of candle wax. There were three candleholders, silver and polished, taken apparently from someone's dining table and carefully placed. Fresh dirt was piled recently over the remains of a corpse, closing up what felt like a wound. The palm of my hand was clutching onto the vines around it.

"It is all right, my girl, if you follow me," the woman said, softly. "You have seen me from the window. Where you live With the man. Hear me talk now. I am present on official business. I am knowing who you are. The rest not my problem. Relax, my girl."

She picked up my hand and held it up to her warm cheek, pointing to the candle wax drippings on the gravestone with the toes in her sandaled foot. She tapped, too, on the fresh dirt piled below it.

She waited until my breathing steadied, and when she was sure I was balanced, Miri took her hand off my face, crossed her arms. Then she started pulling on her discolored lower lip.

"Your mother looking for you, Sette. She ask me: go look for my daughter. And I am looking and reach that monastery with the water tank. I see you are sleeping very nice. With the tall, young man. Then Ada, she knows you are not harmed. I call her, tell her, all is okay, Ada. " Miri paused. "Now look, Sette, I don't have a lot of time right now. But, your mother asked me to look out for you. We are friends a long time indeed, Sette. I know her quite well, many years." I heard a trace of the British accent, of proper British English mixed with the strange Arab intonation in her deep, manly voice. I inspected her shredded leather sandals. Their buckles were broken, and the leather had been treated with linseed oil—I recognized the smell. "We will have buses soon. Buses will drive from this place from the big cities. And carry much clothes and food. Distribute to the people in tents. I have things to give my attention to. Indeed. Not just you, Sette."

The scarring on her chin and cheeks, the discoloring as on her lips, it could have been from the mosquitoes, I thought. Or the sand flies. Her teeth were well cared for. "We got many cats," she rambled on. "In our house in Safat. I named one cat Elijah I know so many Jews. One Jewish girl. She took me to her home. For Passover. This was last year. " Miri clicked her tongue and looked away. "I liked this a lot. "She brushed back her hair with the sinewy, long fingers of her left hand. "Hear me. We could stand here, my girl. Tell stories all night. But, I have business with you now. Then I got to go on into the house I keep in the summers here. Drink some wine, and listen to the radio I don't have time for you. Only."

Miri pointed to a field a few meters away where some ruins of crumbling stone looked like a long- felled tree. "There was a sanatorium, mental hospital for the crazy ones, not far from these graves here. Run then by British. Around here, a famous story. About her brother."

"Whose brother?"

"Ada's brother. In the sanatorium. Had to be sent there when he was just a little older than you, don't know full reason. He hung himself in suicide when he was in the sanatorium. Elizar." She pulled down on her headscarf. She kicked sharply at the stone.

I shifted my weight onto the leg I thought might hold me up better.

"Windy," she said. "My words mean something to you, I hope."

BELOVED ELIZAR SILBERFELD 1918-1948. Drifting into my perception, almost like smoke rings, I absorbed the Hebrew and English lettering. The dates below lopped over the gravestone, under a fringe of white lace, unmistakable in its pattern, and almost pulverized into dust by the bright moonlight. It was the same lace I had seen my mother pull out of a worn trunk up in the attic back in Westchester, a few days before we left for Israel. In a circle where the recess had begun, the knee prints of a kneeling mourner were on the ground.

"Ada's been here. A week ago." Miri said. "When she came she lighted some candles and put some old lace over the grave. Now with the borders, she can't come often. But borders never stop Ada."

Miri bent to scoop some dirt up with her hand.

"Isa, are you sick?" She took some dirt up with her hand.

"No," I said. "I'm not sick. At all."

"I think maybe you are a little. This is not bad. Hasal kheir we say. It means: Good has come about. Now, hear more of the story. Your mother. She was much engaged to famous pediatrician. Name of Dr. Rutherford. From England at the time. Dr. Rutherford was living with your emah's family. In guest room, I do think. Ada finds out he is engaged to another Jewish woman. In Haifa. Your grandfather Wolf throws the doctor's clothes out Ada's window. It was a scandal. Around here. The same year her brother did. Did what he did. The two events, they were too much for your mother. She went on to America. Brawa 'aleisha. Bravo on her."

Miri took a step back from me, no longer making eye contact, and threw the dirt in her hand down. It scattered in the dark wind, and now she was just staring at the air.

"My mother was still alive and young, too. When scandal concerning Elizar happened, she worked for your grandfather. And she loved your mother. Wished she would take better care you know. With the men." Miri looked back at me, "Here I'm the happiest, habibi. I sleep under the moon. My mother also buried. Here. This is how your mother and Miri keep their friendship all these years. Ada comes, lays some stones for her brother. Then we share life. My mother? She got dementia and she died a few ago. I miss her. I come back, do her some bit of honor. I come here in the summers. Like my time alone, too. My face and figure is formidable, but what has been sexual is now talk and memory of mothers. " I only marry once, but he dies of heart attack after third son we have. I am not a lucky woman like Ada. So now Ada and I have much to share again. This summer." She paused. "Well, I telling you a lot, I must know you. Spiritual, it is."

"Please," I let myself interrupt her. "Will you let me telephone my mother from here somewhere?"

"You don't want to telephone, Sette, in case someone else in her house hears, Sette. Ada had to say Elizar was one of the war heroes. Truck comes here from other side, digs up grave and takes Elizar, think he just one of the Jewish soldiers got left behind in Arabic graveyard here like some others, other Jews I mean. This before you were born, when your emah and me we were girls. Now you see, Elizar is just hole in the ground. " Miri put her hand back on my cheek.

Miri stepped towards her shoulder bag, still lying on the dirt where she dropped it. She took an envelope out of it, then removed another keffiyeh out from it. The keffiyeh was blue and pink and made of muslin like her gown. "One of my sons old enough be your twin," she said. Then her teeth made a funny grinding sound, as though she had clicked them, and she lifted up her skirt, and scratched at an itch she had on her calf.

"Put this on, will you? It's a chill out here. She extended the keffiyeh to me. "Your mother knows you are good have health. No telephone. I tell her." She said. Then she handed me the letter, curled my fingers over what I recognized as my mother's handwriting on the translucent envelope.

Miri shook out her legs, one each, after the other, as if all their muscles had stiffened and she was preparing for a long walk.

"I saw Elizar maybe once or twice," she rambled on, talking like my mother did, more to herself than me. "He was a small boy, a small man, not strong. Elizar? His soul goes into a new person, and then it goes into another person and another. Until it is free, I sleep here. Sleep and dream. My mother's skin was smooth, like oil. She smelled like the trees. I sleep with her, all night in a dream together. She has talked to me. Soul is in another person, and then it goes into another person and then another until gets free. That's how it works."

Miri took up a tissue from a pocket on her gown. " Tonight the moon is high and bright. I might settle for some dreams about this place. This night. It is the truth; of course," she said. Then, abruptly: "What you think the Americans will do? I think they will help Israel get the water from the Syrians? I have read in the Post that this man running for president of America in 1964 is named Goldwater." She laughed.

I shook my head.

"Your mother was only in America for a short part of her life. I sleep here like at the grave. Close to her, too, close to your mother, too. The incident with Elizar. It is a worse story. And she plan never come back for years. You understand it, now, Sette. Understand."

"Yes," I said. She was so much like my mother, talking mostly to herself now, I was thinking. And-their likeness was softening all that she was telling me.

"If you talk about things out loud to strangers, not family," she lowered her voice, "the dead cannot come back you know, and be free. Spirit cannot go into next person to be freed. You ruin things if you tell secrets of soul out loud. After your grandfather dies, your mother had gravestone made for Elizar, the fellaheen here helped the Silberfelds put the body in this graveyard here. Silberfelds were a good people, too. You know your mother's mother, Savta, was born in the old city, too."

She finished with a tap of her finger on her chin.

"Go back to the man now," she said. "Not talk to anyone. Things here in the village are different. So how you getting back to the young man?"

I pointed to the way I had come.

"How are you going to walk that way? You can't see anything."

"The moon is full."

"Can I come closer to you?" She asked me suddenly.

I drew back.

"It is too cold out here and I am not a stranger." She said.

I nodded. "Yes; of course, Miri. Absolutely."

She came closer and her fingers flew into my hair.

I tasted the salty run of tears from her eyes

Her finger went up and down my arm. Miri's hand halted near the vein in the crook of my elbow, moved downward to the wrist.

Then, the large uncomforted woman threw her arms around my neck and clung.

When her head bobbed up, our closeness went no further.

She nodded at me, vacantly, then she went to her bicycle, and I watched her climb back on and pedal slowly down the road. She circled back once. "Be careful what you say aloud, Sette." She shouted.

Then she was gone.

Back on the road, the moon -blanched reminders and signposts guided me. I had to keep on the right. I picked my way through the villas under the moonlight.

The night was deep and asleep. There were hardly any stars above. I wanted no more secrets this night. But, I still had the envelope. Through the onionskin, I saw some lira. I could also smell my mother's scents against the shadows the moon, the distant stars.

I took her handwritten note out of the envelope. I read:

Liana, darling. Only come back if you desire. Take some money,
though. I ask of you one thing, my darling. What it is you will
discover there about my life in the past, tell no one.
Your Mommy

In the garden of San Sebastian's, I sat in the bushes alone for a while.
The pine needles and the walnut tree leaves whispered around my legs
and sandaled feet while I surveyed the pathway leading down into the
basement. When I saw William's kerosene light go off, I crept up to the
window and watched the yellowish glow behind the cardboard where
I knew William was reading by his cigarette lighter or a candle. More
about kayak signals. The fan was whirring.

In the dark, I saw his awkward boat, its cockpit painted yellow now,
William had been able to sandpaper its hull until it looked slick and
shiny. A wooden rudder secured on its rear.

I heard a scratching noise in the distance. Stray cats again, under the
leaves, trying to warm themselves. He was waiting for me, I knew, he
was restless even with his eyes steadyfast on the kayak manual.

I wanted to move towards William, to tell him what had happened.
To take his arm in both my hands as he sat, looking downward into his
kayak guide, with the fan blowing into his hair, and the wick of his cigarette lighter burning down between his fingers.

But, I put my mother's letter down, safely to the ground.

Beyond were the vines, the water tank. And when reached the tank
instead, I climbed up its rusty side ladder. Walnut leaves floated in the
water, the water that was thick as the Dead Sea and, under the moonlight, looked nearly milky.

The water inside the tank was unattended and had become filled
with debris from the garden. Flowers had dropped in too, and the
water level was up to the top. I lifted off my shirt and skirt as I heard

the wind stirring some bits of leaves from the surface of the water. The ripples were silky despite the debris in them.

Then on the last notch of the ladder I fell into the tank, plunging down into the water. My feet scraped against the rough bottom, and then I splashed and floated up. The moonlight fell like sun as it dried my cheeks, but the dirty water burned. I could not blink away the silt on my eyelids, but I went down another time, into the thick water. I popped up, surfaced again, and finally pulled myself out of the tank. My mother might have been out in the night with me, asking me didn't I want to come back to her? In this wild impulse in the night, I had found something of her again.

Gradually, I climbed down the outside ladder. The earth beneath was dry and beaten and littered with wrappers, and the empty cigarette boxes Jordanian military patrols threw from their jeeps as they whizzed past our cellar.

Picking my mother's letter back up from the ground I tracked my way back to the cellar wondering what would happen if I just turned and went back to Metaduleh Street, back to the limestone house.

William was in bed fast asleep when I got back. The cellar was dark; his cigarette lighter was on the floor. The fan was still whirring, sounding like a bird caught in heavy wind. My clothes gave off a stench, drying. I pulled a night dress on. It was too dark to see the stains on my face from the rank water inside the tank, but I squinted, hoping the darkness would offer up some image from which I could grasp the feelings inside me.

I tugged on the night dress and the clutching earth crusting between my fingers brought me the memory of my mother's body. I patted at my hair and its dripping slippery film, at things invisible, ghost skin.

Under the sheets with William, I felt my head throbbing, my nightdress sticking to my thighs, sweat running now between my breasts, behind my knees. I couldn't sleep.

I wanted some chocolate. My head was swimming, but I could not bring myself to sit up and lean against the cellar wall. It wasn't that I was hungry, but the desire for one of my mother's chocolate bars gnawed at me until I felt tears.

The liquid from the water tank had dried as flakes, crusting the inside of my legs and producing a flavor in the air that I breathed in and tasted, like warm egg white, or a wash done on my skin with a tongue-licking that I wanted to keep.

I would wash in the morning, I decided.

I would have liked to light a candle. But that would awaken William. I covered myself with the topsheet, deciding I would tell him in the morning about Miri and Elizar's grave, my mother's letter. I had stashed the lira and my mother's letter in the makeshift closet under some skirts when I undressed, but I felt my stomach unhinge now.

I crept closer to William under the sheets, drifting into half-sleep, hearing the fan, then from this sound, I began hearing a myriad of sounds—murmurs, voices, whispers of darkness, water, gravestones. Voices evocative of names and times and places of which I had been conscious all my life without really thinking about them. I drifted further, into smelling the cocktails and fried pita bread of a party in the ballroom of the King David Hotel. I heard the bells of a grandfather clock strike ten. The characters in the ballroom stepped from the paintings of the old and departed in the house at Metadulah Street, the watercolor portraits hanging on the whitewashed walls over the dining room table.

Sounds of laughter, and clinking wine glasses swelled all around me in the King David ballroom and up against a wall in the corner opposite me, I saw my mother. She moved about, short and full, in an open room exquisite with the beauty of old Palestine. The doors and windows were engraved with mystical, scrolling marble work; the ceilings high, and the chandeliers looked new and diamondy. Now in her first youth, my mother, with a pile of reddish brown hair clumsily tucked into a truss, became more compelling the longer I watched. I saw a man whisper in her ear, touch her shoulder, toy with her hair. She was laughing, and I was so happy. I liked it here, I loved her here. When the man took her hand, held her fingers, then I was safe from her voracity, her hunger. I started to come out from my corner. I wanted to reach for her.

She felt it too. If it were not for the tangle of sorrow all around us, we might have crumpled into each other's arms, mother and daughter. But, my mother smoothed out her green silk dress, and I awoke.

The room was silent. I blinked my eyes, and with a wash of dawn light from the outside window, the room's objects swam back into view. The kayak, the makeshift closet in the corner, the fan.

I stared up at the shredded pictures of the Saints on the old scarred walls. Through the muslin curtains, the dawn sun was blinding, like a strong strobe light.

My hand darted out to feel William's body beside me. Then sitting up in bed, dressed in the smock dress, I propped myself against the wall wondering what William was dreaming; his hands clasped to the sides of his body.

For the next few days, William started bringing the kayak out to the garden so we could work on it under the better light.

In the distance, small black birds hovered over the fields, fighting the winds rolling up from the desert. The bald, dry earth bore the blaze started in the fields by the farmers, and after the shrubs burnt, and the already sun-charred blades of grass, the stone, and rocks themselves could not burn.

It was the locusts the farmers had been after; William later explained.

That whole next week, William had not been so animated since he told me about the storks. If the locusts touch each other's thighs, flick flick flick (William demonstrated by flicking the fingernail of his fore-finger on his thumbnail) rub rub rub (he rubbed his thigh with the flat of his right hand) swarms that sound like jet planes in the sky grow, he said staring upwards. And before you know it, the locusts have gnawed and ravaged every blade of grass, every flower, and fruit from the soil.

Only the wind can save us, blowing them to the sea to drown. Heaps of dead grasshoppers otherwise pile up in the fields. The fellaheen have to burn them. William had heard these stories from the other farmers.

All through our last nights together, our radio played news about the hostilities. From a long distance, down by the border, and only a few kilometers from where I remembered my grandmother's house and the pine forest, came billows of smoke.

My mother had been good as her word, never sending a message again. I told myself I would at least write her a letter soon. There were days I missed her terribly.

I did not tell William about meeting Miri. Or what I learned about Elizar. Or about my mother's letter. If I truly believed Miri—that in telling the secret out loud, the probation of whatever soul was within all of us would never finish, I didn't know. I simply did not tell William. I tried to many times, when we ate and slept together. But only a forbidding silence came between us.

One early morning, William finally unroped the finished kayak from its homemade rigging. The weather was burning hot.

I stood stationed by the water tank, feeling the morning margarine, and flat bread still between my teeth from our breakfast, as William dragged the six feet kayak across the garden walk to the gate. Its stern bumped and scraped on the stone.

I broiled him some eggs outside in the garden on a slab of stone I had learned to lay on top of the Bunsen burner. The stone got so hot I turned the eggs over with his army knife, careful not to puncture the opaque albumen, the yolk the bright yellow of a gum drop back home. He sat under the dawn sun, eating and figuring out the factors of the coming kharmsin winds.

"Look William," I said that morning, holding the book he had given me. A manual on kayak signals in the wilderness. I touched my forehead with the index finger of my right hand. The signal for 'me' in the manual.

"Where did you learn that?" He asked me.

"I learned it." I said.

He put down his plate of eggs. He took a heave of breath and pointed his index fingers at his chest. "What's it mean?"

"I, me," I said.

"Good. What's this?" He whipped his index finger across his throat.

"It means: Let's quit. Cut it."

"Good, Liana. That's good. What about this?"

"Relax." I tried to smile, but William put his fist in the air.

"And this? This means stop, hold position."

"I knew that." I said.

William stepped back, as if on a stage about to perform the hardest magic trick. "Okay, here we go. What's this. Liana?" He took three fingers and held them limp over his right ear. "Well?"

"I don't know."

"This?" He repeated the gesture.

"I forgot, William."

"I told you last night, before you went to bed."

"I know, but I forgot."

William made the signal for "pay attention" again, waving his left arm over his head. "That one you forgot is the one you should remember because it's made for you." He eased his arm back down.

We went on a trial run with the kayak before it got dark, William carrying it on his shoulders, when I couldn't even lift it from the ground.

We walked up the path where the burning fire around the water tank had left charred cacti that now looked like charcoal.

"We're not going to take the road," William said, "We have to get through the thickets where we won't be spotted. They lead to the same field. If we go around the trees there," William pointed straight ahead, at a barren spot with no signs of footprints or traffic. "We are on our way to the ledges overlooking Jericho. It's at least two kilometers down to the river from there." We trudged far through the wild land that day. We walked east, to the scorched mountain ledge.

Finally tired, William put the heavy kayak down. He bent to the dusty ground, and I looked down at the valley.

That night, I settled down with the kayak book and my journal. I propped myself up on the sill, with the radio blasting a new Beatle song. I read through some of my journal entries.

July 16: The kayak is done and there is little to do but wait for the time to leave. And follow the newspaper reports. William was quiet as I took the sheets to wash in the water tank this evening. He took his books outside to the garden. I caught him staring in the window, with cloudy eyes.

July 20: The cellar smells of kerosene lamps today, olive leaves and jasmine. We drank some wine in the evening. Without saying so, William let me know I was doing well with my Arabic. and French.

July 21: He went over to where his kayak was and pulled up a sheet he must have washed for us in the rain with soap. He leaned his head into my face and I felt his breath against my chest. He pulled in closer to me. When he kissed me, I believed in God

It's way past midnight and William is sleeping.

July 22. (I copied this from an old THE GUIDE TO ISRAEL booklet I found in the corner of the monastery):

'There is no country in the world, so varied in experience as Israel. The changes that transformed mankind took place here at the source and core of ancient history. Here, too converge various biological and phytogeographcial zones of the world. In the land of Israel you behold a nation of remnants gathered from all parts of the world restored to a new life.'

Laying the manual, out on my knees I read tried to study the kayak signals from one of William's:

"Miscellaneous Signals

BYE: a wave good bye—end transmission; good bye

GOT IT: form a circle with thumb & index—A-okay; I understand

GREETING: give Vulcan greeting—live long and prosper

HAIL: lightly wave arm over head—hail; listen up

HELP: strongly wave arm over head—-help; assistance needed

NO: shake head from side to side—no; I disagree

WHAT: place palm up near shoulder—
who/where/when/how/wanna?

WILL COMPLY: salute—I understand and will comply

YES: shake head up and down—yes; I agree

UNSURE: rotate down palm from side to side—not sure; can't decide; iffy. . . . "

It was dawn outside when William and I left our monastery a few days later. "July 27th", and I was dressed in my bluejeans skirt and sandals. We walked down the road and turned on a wild path to the Rift. We decided that last night it was time for our return, but that I would return to my mother, back home. I had already known somewhere that he would not let me go to Jericho with him.

In the fields, it was already the usual morning, hot and stifling. Shots were fired from somewhere over a horizon that was smokeless, devoid of any fire but the round ball of the rising sun.

After a while, we stopped. We hadn't had anything for breakfast but Nescafe and tomatoes. William reached in his duffel bag and brought out the two sandwiches I had wrapped in newspaper the night before. The brine of the goat cheese dripped onto his giant fingers, and he licked them. "Take one of these. Sit down for a moment and eat. We'll talk. You're anxious."

I took the other sandwich.

He started eating, standing up, rolling his tongue over his lips, looking thirsty from the salt of the cheese, the hard work of walking.

"We should have got some beer from the farmers," he said. "You know the route back to Jerusalem, we've gone over it a long time."

"Yes," I said, and I dropped my sandwich. Then, picking it up again, I began unwrapping it, slowly sitting down on the scorched yellow grass.

"Was it One Metadulah? That is the address of your grandmother's house, isn't it?" He asked. I nodded.

Then William edged, by stages, onto the grass beside me. "We don't have much time here," he said. "When the sun fully rises, we can be seen."

I stayed, seated on the grass staring into the chunks of white cheese in my sandwich.

William's hands were hot and raw on the sides of my face. Then his mouth punched into my lips like a blow. I opened my mouth and felt his tongue, the shock of the pungent cheese inside my throat. I stared at a heat rash on his neck, a red mark irregular as the shape of a continent, as he drew his tongue along the roof of my mouth, his lips still fastened onto mine.

I felt the tips of his fingers on my shirt, my breasts, and then, dropping the sandwich again, my hand went to his groin. I felt the hard curve between his thigh and his hip, the rising and swell of my excitement.

"No," he said, quickly taking my hand. He held it inside his fingers, shaking his head. He moaned, but it was tenderness I heard from his lips. He was not quite real, my avatar from the land of ghosts.

His eyes now released me, enveloped me again though he was sending me back to my mother. Looking into his eyes, I saw myself as something floating in an immense pool. His face was smooth, and wide, and I imagined starry things: there were stray cats in his hand, he was saving them from themselves and the hot sun and the fact that they do not exist.

He waited a few moments before he let go of my hands and stood. And then, I waited for him to tell me when he was to begin his walk to the ledge.

"I need to go now," he finally said.

I stood up, and some of the pleasure William hadn't wanted me to feel dashed over me. Tears licked at my cheeks, too, rolling across to my earlobes, but they were small and glimmery.

William cleaned up our picnic with a towel from his duffel bag. He spent a few minutes unfurling one of the elaborate charts he had made in the cellar with his blueprints, and I saw him actually making small notes with his Bic pen like some mission had been completed.

I watched him put his "calculations" back in his duffel bag, lace a belt back around his jeans and then check through his binoculars, trying to see whether anyone had come up the path while he wasn't thinking of it. Once he was sure we hadn't been seen, he came to me and put out his hand.

"Liana," he said.

The morning was spectacular with a full orange sunrise. The arid air felt as it always had. Miles below us, the city of Jericho slept. Distant groves and mounds streaked the sediment with the reddish color of a rich henna.

William lifted the kayak onto his back. Then he was gone.

I followed a trail back to the monastery, low morning clouds hovering over me. The path cut through a dense grove of pine trees and I followed it, riding the bright sunlight breaking through branches.

The morning had started over the fields.

There were some dried orange trees on the bank and the cows and goats walked loose, grazing on the yellow grass. Almonds fell from the dwindling almond trees along the road to the Allenby Bridge, the way to Amman.

Overhead, an airplane flew and a siren sounded by the borders.

The sound of the winds scraping in the dirt of the path was startling, raw.

I felt the wind brush the denim of my skirt. The material had turned almost bone- colored, washed in tank water over and over again. But in the new sunlight, it looked like blue quartz.

I heard a muezzin from the mosque far away, in the opposite direction. Some of the religious farmers had gone to chant at the mosque in Ramallah, leaving their huts locked up.

Back on the road, I continued to count the reminders and faded signposts.

Soon, I got thirsty. At the first set of huts and old deserted houses perched on a hill, I traveled up a narrow path of broken shrubs and vines, hoping to find a store or kiosk selling orange soda. I didn't recognize the camp. I stopped after a few minutes and rested my back, reaching a scabby wall of one of the ruined Arabic houses. It was peeling so badly I could see the raw sandstone underneath. I put down my knapsack and swallowed in some of the warm air. All the vaulted alleyways of the camp were closed.

I thought of hearing my mother's voice over the phone. Of, how simple it would be if I were in Westchester. Would anything be different when I went back to her? I thought I heard someone coming, but it was the UN flag waving over a shut kiosk.

Then, from between scraps of light I saw a woman come out to the porch of her hut, sweeping it with her broom. She was lean and small and bent over, pushing at the accumulating mud after the long dawn. The headlights of a car lighted up a distant cafe. I continued walking. When I got close enough to a cafe, I saw two men were playing backgammon and sipping coffee from silver cups.

Then I could smell the closed fish markets. A few of the Arabs were shopping in the unkempt vaulted alley I had reached, Bedouin stalls at the end of a dusty street. A sign was posted by a large blue UN flag waving at the top of a tall pole. There were flies buzzing above sticky stalls that were like a donkey shacks, different shops selling fruits, and house supplies.

I went inside the first stall I saw with groceries. Under its shaky roof, there were piles of staples—rice, dried peas and lima beans. Contest forms for a 1960 Miss Schlitz Beer Contest in Milwaukee were stacked with worn paper-thin books in Arabic on Amman and Jordan's other cities. They were so old the shopkeeper wrapped them in newspaper to shelter the pages, the bindings. Opened crates were loaded up with containers of black tooth powder, laxatives, witch hazel, bottles of mineral water, cans of peas and gravies.

"I will be getting a whole box of Pepsi Cola soon," the bearded, shawled man said to me." You come in the month August, it will be here."

"Thank you," I said.

"Would you like to come more inside?" He asked me. I followed him as he pulled some bright blue curtains apart and went with him to the hidden back room with a window. There, he had a backgammon set on a marble table, beautiful china, and Turkish water pipes. His wife sat on a reed mat roasting watermelon seeds in a pan of oil that sent up a plume of salty smoke, the burning nut smell intoxicating. The old woman in black was also swatting at the mosquitoes between stacks of cauliflowers.

"English?" She asked me after the shopkeeper left us alone, to go back to selling his goods in the front.

"American. I am looking for some tomatoes." "Student?"

"No, no."

"Welfare worker, yes? From United Nations."

"I am not," I said. Her fleshy body brought me back to the memory of my mother, to the closeness I had become to fear again, thinking of seeing my mother without William.

"Hot?" She asked me, tapping at the white handkerchief, tied under her chin. The woman must have felt my anxiety. She took out a towel, shook it out, beat it with her hand, tossed and smacked it, then extended it to me, pointing to my head, and then to the ceiling: "Sun. Hot. Wear."

I took the towel from her hands and wrapped it over my hair. The woman shooed away the flies whirling over her roasting pans. She kept her load of giant cauliflowers there, by her roasting pans, the cauliflowers were big as boulders. They looked like moon bushes.

Two boys scrambled inside the room, their legs were tawny, scabby. "*Yallah* . . ." The boys let her run her chapped finger over their faces, then take their heads between her hands, bending them down. She kissed the dusty black hair. She had change for them in a tiny silver bowl. They pocketed the shiny coins, and raced around her excited, shouting: "*Todah rah bah. Todah*!"

When the boys left, she pulled out the thick metal pot from the corner of the room, and, running some water into it, put it on an old primus, lighting it with a match. Then she spooned out some espresso coffee with a silver teaspoon, let the espresso fall into the pot about to boil. She clinked the spoon against the metal, lowered the heat. The whole room began to smell like aromatic charcoal.

We sat cross-legged on the floor in silence until the water boiled, and then she rose, poured two demitasse cups with the coffee, spooning into each five or six teaspoons of crystal sugar. She brought them over to me, blowing on the cups to cool the bubbling brown-black liquid.

I took one of the steaming cups and sipped. The sediment of coffee grounds at the bottom of my cup was thick and delicious as candy. I thought of my mother, the two of us drinking orange soda again on the porch at Metadulah, of her asking me to lie with her on the salon couch. I stared at a spot by the old woman's skirt one of the boys had squatted to get his coins. And, for the first time, I thought of the young Arab child in the tree, high and dangling before the shots. What would I feel if I only was returning to the way my life had been before?

"Finish." The old woman stood near me, sipping her own cup.

After some moments, when she turned her transistor radio on and the Arabic music sounded, I picked up a loose sheet of cardboard and a pencil her husband must have used to mark his crates. I sketched her the face of the soft; curly-headed Arabic boy we had nearly forgotten. I outlined his nose, his ears on some rough brown paper with the black crayon she used to mark her crates.

"You know him, please?" I asked her. "I have been looking for his parents. A long time."

"You?" She said to me, as if pleased she had finally sensed my distress after all these minutes had passed." No, no, *habibi.*"

She suddenly sprang over to the crates. She squatted above a tray of vegetables from one of the crates, her full skirt billowing covering it. Carefully, her fingers went under her skirt selecting vegetables. When she pulled them out, onto her lap, she was caressing them with her fingers. She put them to her dusty lips like the heads of the boys.

"You, no boy. You—" She tossed the two cucumbers to the back wall to reach under her massive skirt again. She pulled out a blood-red tomato and shook it at me. "You—this," she pointed to her groin.

Then she put the luscious plump tomato in my palms, closing my fingers around it.

"You no, *habibi,*" she said and threw her head back and laughed until she shook out a shock of her hair from her scarf.

I held the tomato under the sun when I left the stall.

My denim wrap-a-round blew about me and rippled in the breezes. It felt supernatural; such happiness. I don't remember how I knew which trail to follow to get back to One Metadulah. I kept the towel wound on my head under the burning sun.

The pine needles and the walnut tree leaves whispered around my legs and sandaled feet while I surveyed the pathway. I heard a motorbike on its way to the old city, faraway. I walked thinking of my mother's earthy, silent grace at the King David Hotel, in the house at Metadulah Street, and all the lies.

Then in a clearing under the carob trees, I saw the black storks for the first time in Jordan; the same black storks William and I had seen before we crossed over the border. The rattling of their bills sounded like a hundred squalling infants. With their red, peely eyes, they appeared almost sickly, but their heads, neck and back wings shone with iridescent reflections.

The bushes were almost translucent, dried of their green. There were crows on the brittle branches of dying ficus trees. White butterflies fluttered around the vines, but the path was rough with thistles, and fat lizards slithered between rocks and boulders.

I kept walking, knowing the direction. I didn't know why but somewhere on that road, I let everything go.

I walked, thinking about my mother. But how now, like the women here before me, I had my secrets and my romance.

I felt an ache in my belly and heard a Peter, Paul, and Mary song playing in my head, which had been on the radio yesterday. I wondered where Elizar's grave was, if it was like the others, anonymous— the headstone eaten by heat and years. I saw him alive when I closed my eyes for a second. Elizar with his thin, desperate face, his glaring eyes in which burned indomitable desire. I envisioned his skull, and the piece of collar bone he had cracked and tugged off by hanging himself, the eye holes of death staring back, risen from the ground.

Then, as if I had seen something clearer for the first time, I wasn't scared of loving my mother anymore. Running from her, I had only traveled deeper into her, embracing her borderland with wide arms.

Had my mother really meant to take me so far away from known boundaries? Her desperate longings to be the only world defining us, my body and its life?

She had been unable to deal with the same disappointment again. It had been too close to her disgrace and secrets, the suicide of my father.

Phantom winds blew her back to me with no demands except to feel her strength again. But by midnight, from a great distance beyond barbed wire and warning posts, my grandmother's hammock finally glinted before my eyes. I bent under it, crawling, crossing the border again—back into the world I had come from.

5

In 1986, I went back to Israel with my husband. I wanted to show him the land that had formed me. My mother lived in New York City by then, but she went back every few years to visit Doda Esther and attend various occasions with her old friends. Jerusalem had been cold that February day.

My husband and I took a sherut from Ben-Gurion airport, following the glistening route which passed new-sprung Jewish settlements and towns full of jerrybuilt apartment houses. New gray buildings were everywhere, renovations in progress—teams of back hoes and bulldozers lay in wet mud. Israeli checkpoints were now bulletproof closures with reinforced steel doors.

The highway through the Judean Hills was unrecognizable, except for the rusted tanks and Fords from the War of Independence that were still cradled in heaps of shrubs and rocks. The sky that morning looked bruised by the lowering winter clouds, my mother was no longer here to enchant the stonescape and clay; the lavender was dark.

Soon, the gardens of Jerusalem appeared outside our window; crocuses and Jerusalem roses drowned in floods of thawing ice. The air was raw and cruel, scratchy, the biting wind didn't flag, and there had been more rainfall than the land could soak in. Vapors fumed from the sodden fields, drenched city benches. Some blue Arabic villages lay behind blocked hillocks on the West Bank, closed-off, their rickety watchtowers overlooking the barren soil I remembered. The borders were marked only by yellow warning road signs in English, Hebrew, and Arabic which pointed towards Jordan.

The monastery still existed somewhere, I believed, in the far away, impoverished vista of limestone and dust.

I brushed my hand against the window to clear a vision of a ravaged distant land.

Entering the center of the new city, a light snow began to fall. The snowflakes looked like mixed salt and powder.

The old tailor shop and one pharmacy were deserted hovels in rubble, the places I remembered walking with my mother to buy toothpastes that smelled like lemons and aspirin pills the size of playing dice. The harsh metallic feel I remembered in the Jerusalem air was gone, the snow melted in the sand and stone heaps, it drizzled into the abandoned alleys, a white liquid painting shapes and ghostly forms.

I sank into my seat, wondering if it would have turned out different for me had I known long ago what the war for the water would become. If I had known the border skirmishes as different from the rage and struggle inside me. Would I have decided to go to the Israeli police station instead, in my old army shorts and sandals, reporting the death I still saw in my night dreams with the young Arab's face? He had my own face back then, too, my physical confusions, my formlessness.

Soldiers in olive uniforms still guarded the bus stops with heavy rifles. They walked in groups on the new sidewalks now, clicking against each other. It was rush hour on King George Street. The boulevard was filling with cars and red buses. Lines of Israelis were forming at the kiosks to buy lotto tickets, municipal parking tickets, chewing gum, and stamps.

Ahead, the King David Hotel shone as if rebuilt into polished white steel.

My eyes blinked, spotting a Thai restaurant in a strip of modern boutiques.

When the door to my grandmother's house at One Metadulah Street opened, it was Doda Esther who embraced me.

"Liana," she said, the same hefty, strong woman I remembered. "Who would have supposed," she teased, "Liana married." Immediately, she lifted up my suitcase. "*Kah-hah, kah-hah,*" she commanded, carrying it and motioning for my husband and me to follow her up the marble stairway, as if we were still children. "Come and later go downstairs to drink something. We have Diet Pepsi-cola you know."

Doda Esther was living alone on the second level which had been converted into her separate quarters. Savta had died in 1970, Dod Yakov had died of a heart attack in 1982. My cousin had come back with three children and her own husband. They lived downstairs where Savta's bedroom and the salon had been.

After unpacking that evening I went to see Doda Esther lying in her bed, inside the bedroom where Yakov and she used to sleep together. She was looking out the window at the moon amid the shifting clouds. Blue shadows moved over her.

I went to the window to look out, too. Three or four tall new stone apartment buildings obstructed the view. Faded Israeli flags hung over high terraces. There was no way to see the pine forest or the fields. Or the spot of the killing now.

"Beautiful sky, isn't it?" Doda Esther asked, wistfully. "Yes," I said.

"And my sheets are so soft, darling. Really." I moved back from the window to her. She turned her head towards me. "And your Mommy, she is well in New York?"

"Yes, Doda."

"That was nice when you came to visit as a young girl, wasn't it?" She smiled.

"Yes," I said again, letting her kiss me. I could feel her thinking, weighing, deciding what to say next.

She suddenly looked very tired, her gray skin and her brown eyes wrinkled. "Very nice," she said.

When letters came to my grandmother's house that August of 1963, I had raked through them, searching for William's large, clumsy writing. But I had found none. My aunt finally told me this visit in 1986 that she had received some strange letters she never gave to me. Too much had happened, she said. And the name on the return envelope had been illegible. The paper was soiled by swamp and dust. "Ada did after all call that old friend of hers in Safad to look out for you. What was her name? Oh, yes, now I remember, Miri." Doda Esther told me one afternoon that February of 1986. "The parents of the American boy you stayed with came to the house. Very nice. Your mommy gave them cafe and biscuits in the salon. Of course, they discussed very well what must be done. That you not have to face the authorities. The American boy, he had a very nice father. Charming, I thought. They are in America now, don't you think? We did not keep in touch. Of course. We organized the plans together to keep everything—how do you say it—to *our-self* I think you say in English." I wasn't surprised by this sudden telling so many years later. Or that the Coons had come to speak to my mother. There had been no more in the Israeli papers about an "abducted" American diplomat's son, or any mention of William's further whereabouts after I had returned.

I would miss Metadulah Street and this house, I realized now. "Your Mommy is not a woman without virtues you know, darling," my aunt added and I swallowed, remembering all that had happened.

That long ago August, a deep pain had fisted around my stomach, squeezing it. The outpouring had been in a fever. When the mass of tissues and blood first leaked to the bathroom floor, exuding a metallic stench, the blood was black and it clotted like a clumpy syrup, then smelled like earth.

My mother had stood me up over the toilet hole, white towels in her hand. She brought my screaming face to her bosom. "You're just having a miscarriage, sweetheart," she kept saying, holding one of the towels out like a tiny trampoline under my womb. She brought hot milk and honey to me in bed after cleaning me with witch hazel.

The chaos still oozed out from inside me in the night and daily she washed the sheets with the water she and Doda Esther had saved for emergencies.

Doda Esther had masterly ushered an elderly doctor into the bedroom where I had lain with my headaches, my numbness, and despair. The rest of the time at Metadulah Street had been cloaked in silence. We had Friday night dinners, and Savta taught me how to play the Israeli version of gin rummy with Zorah, Esther, and my mother. Ivy went back to America before my mother and me to make it in time for school that fall of 1963. She sent me some bottles of Southern Comfort from the duty-free shop at Idlewild. If my mother knew where William was, or who he was, she never told the police either. We did not talk about him at all after a while. The unspoken loyalty of some long ago code. Of how the rules worked in this place.

Perhaps William believed I had stopped caring about him when he received no replies to his letters.

One morning, two days before departing again for America, I left my husband sleeping in our bed sheets. I tiptoed down the long stairway to the foyer. I opened the bumpy glass doors to the salon and stepped again onto the musty red carpet, recognizing the stuffy odors of lemony cleaning fluids and polished pewter. At the sliding glass window where I had once watched the dawn come, my mother finally asleep beside me on the same couch that stood there now.

I tried to remember it as it had been to me in 1963—a geography, undifferentiated, hungry for definition, wanting water. I peered out at the dun-colored terrain, at all the borders and boundaries still so explosive and fragile. In my dreams sometimes I still smelled the white dirt of the fields, the earth and its bones. I remembered how I had once felt as thirsty as the land. So much like me, I thought, a fragile mistress.

The view towards Jordan was obstructed now as it was from my aunt's room upstairs, apartment houses in the way of my vision. I could not see the path in the old forest where I first met William either, or the leafy grave of the slain boy we never reported, leaving him there to lie in the dry, brittle soil.

The building of the Israeli Water Works project was just beginning when my mother, and I left Jerusalem the spring of 1964. By 1965, the hostilities along the forty-seven-mile frontier between Syria, Jordan, and Lebanon were growing into one the Middle East's most unrelenting border wars.

I went to sit in the salon couch where I had slept a night long ago with my mother. I felt the warm cushion, remembering the intoxication of her flesh. I felt something awful and magical and potent as the stars acting out the larger world of military stations and barbed wires around the territories of identity.

I wonder how a girl loves her mother, if not by an enchantment which a strange man mysteriously breaks and repossesses one day.

From one-thirty p.m.until five that day, as my husband went with Doda Esther to the new concert hall by the post office for a "cinema," I stayed up in the bedroom.

The closet door was left open, and I could see there were cricket balls and hatboxes and cashmere sweaters on shelves, with the stacks of old British romance novels. Tattered paperbacks were piled atop old khaki Bermuda shorts and worn hiking boots. Photos of my mother in the Haganah, the Jewish underground. Here was an army green knapsack she had once strapped on her shoulders. Her old water canteens still smelled of oranges and sweat. There were no photos of Elizar. But, a young Doda Esther waved at the camera in a black-and-white still, her long black braids went all the way down to her hips.

Some of the dresses and undergarments were on the closet floor. I recognized the stockings she wore that summer of 1963, one of her girdles. A tiny closet dresser was built into the corner of the closet, and I opened a drawer, pulling out one of the brassieres she must have left behind, too, when we packed that late August to return to America. I held the bra up, the loop of its straps in both my hands. The bra's cups felt warm in the enclosure of space. There was a wire pushed all around the two cups. I looked at the reflection in the mirror on the inside of the closet's door, then into the prickly darkness that surrounded them, holding the cups in front of my breasts. The old white lace made my skin seem darker, my head look smaller, and the bra cups were as large as my thighs which looked more rounded as they stood under the awning of my mother's garment.

What would have happened if I had never gone with William to the monastery?

I turned on the hanging light bulb and looked hard at my body. I slipped my arms through the straps, and the bra slipped down my chest, falling. I fastened the four metal clasps in the back and brought it up again, over my breasts. I pushed the cups, and the pearl-white fabric slackened, the huge phantom breasts caving in. The bra wasn't padded; nothing was padded in my mother's country. But elemental and old. Slowly, I inhaled a sweet familiar odors of secrets and skin.

Took them in. Inside the closet, the smells were as powerful as if an aromatic oil had spilled.

Then, in his deep clear voice, I imagined William saying: *Undress now. You are not such a bad person.*

Afterword

A DEDICATION IN MEMORIAM TO GRACE PALEY:

"That eye with which any artist looks at life is really dumb in a lot of ways," Grace Paley told Paul Wilner of the New York Times in 1979. "Some people prefer to call it innocent because that makes it classier, in a little way, but it's really just dumb. I'm an ear believer. I think the ear is smarter than the eye."

I HAD THE GIFT OF STUDYING WITH GRACE PALEY as an undergraduate at Sarah Lawrence and later as a graduate student. I was in the classroom when the Times came to take Grace's photograph that day in 1979. Looking back to those college days, I realize that even the thought I could ever write anything even resembling a novel was remote and ridiculous to me for many reasons. Besides, a total lack of skill and self-confidence, the door to my memory room had become unhinged by an increasing loss of visual reference points both within myself and among the people who would receive my work. My Jewish great grandmother, grandmother, and mother were all born in the ancient city of Jerusalem in a multicultural Palestine of Muslims, Christians, and Jews. Most potential readers, I thought and perhaps still believe, wouldn't even know there had been a world before the state of Israel was formed in

1948 or that this world included Jews, including many non-zionist Jews who coexisted peacefully with their Arab neighbors.

For Grace, the years-long struggle of the marginalized and the not yet heard to bring their voices to the literary sound stage was a rite of passage that built the inner strength a writer needed to develop anyway. Grace was the master of telling stories about the marginalized, so good that "marginalized" became for me not an awful word, but a special place of privilege.

The news about Israel and the war there was constant throughout my lifetime, but after the first Infatida in the 1980s, bombings and death were graphically shown on TV in monotonous, bloody, relentless, and repeated reportage. Because Grace was political, Israel began to gain prominence in her own life. I phoned her daily, telling her stories, sharing the intimate scenes of sitting around the dinner table in 1963, in early Jerusalem when my mother took me there to visit as a child. These stories seemed to illuminate a forgotten Jerusalem, not so besieged and terrifying.

On September 11th, 1991, Grace Paley wrote on my behalf to the United Nations. Through her support, I was able to meet and interview the UN Mandate representative of Palestine. From there, the chaotic birth of this novel began.

Eventually, my first novel Edges, O Israel, O Palestine got written. In May, 2005, even more miraculously, Grace Paley herself, at the age of 82, edited and then published it through her own Glad Day Books, a publishing house her husband, Robert Nichols started to bridge the gap between imaginative literature and political articles and criticism which have been fixed under the labels of "Fiction" and "Nonfiction." This split, Grace said, diminished literature and it usefulness to society. Grace, terribly ill then with cancer, even lugged the manuscript to the printer, going over every word with her pitch-perfect ear.

The last conversation I had with Grace, only two weeks ago today, included telling her that the novel had been optioned by Triboro Pictures for feature film, to be shot on location in my mother's native city, a now-divided Jerusalem. Grace and I decided that what we wanted to do with some of the proceeds was start an archive at the Jerusalem museum of first person accounts from other families, Arabs and Jews, whose lives, like mine, were full of erased stories of friendship and affinity. Grace died on August 22 at her home in Vermont.

It is my greatest privilege to dedicate this book to her now, my literary mother, mentor, and friend who will, for me and so many other continue to teach us that our ears are smarter than we think, and our eyes can forever embrace the light she left glowing for us in the dark.

—LEORA SKOLKIN-SMITH SEPTEMBER 2007

About the Author

B ORN IN MANHATTAN IN 1952, Leora spent her childhood between New York and Israel, traveling with her family to her mother's birthplace in old Jerusalem every three years. She has been published in Persea: An International Review and the Sarah Lawrence Review. The recipient of grants from The Department of Cultural Affairs, the New York State Council on the Arts, and P.E.N. American Center, she has also developed and directed writing programs for the mentally ill in eight major psychiatric hospitals. In the last few years she was co-founder of The Emmett Till/Anne Frank program, a multicultural educational initiative for Afro-American and Jewish youth in Brooklyn. Leora holds a B.A. and M.F.A. from Sarah Lawrence College. This is her first published full-length novel.

Glossary of Hebrew Words

(All transliterations by Lilly Rivlin)

achshav (now)
Americanit (American person)
aaz (so)
beh-vaka-shah (please)
beit (house)
Dod (uncle)
Doda (aunt)
Giveret (prefix for "Mrs.")
Giverot (plural of Giverat)
ha-yom (today)
he (she)
ka-ha (like this)
ken (yes)
kloom (nothing)
lashevet (sit down)
lo (no)
ma-ka -rah (what's the matter?)
ma-shlomecha-mech (how are you?) (feminine)
ma-shlomo-mech (how are you?)
mawtek (darling)
ma -yesh (what do you want?)
ma-zeh (what's this?)
me-od (very much)
meshugaeem (fools) (the crazy)
mevinah (understand)
nichmad me'od (very nice)
nichmad (nice)
po (here)
Shalom (hello, goodbye, peace)

182 Leora Skolkin Smith

shama (over there)
shel-lee (mine) (feminine)
shel-lo (yours) (masculine)
shel-lach (yours) (feminine)
Sette (Arabic for "Miss")
todah (thank you)
todah reh-bah (thank you very much)
tov (good)
yaldah (girl)
yeled (boy)
yoffee (terrific! or: wonderful!)
yom (day)
who (he)
zeh (here)
zoozy (move)

TRANSJORDAN

"The Emirate of Transjordan (Arabic: Im rat Sharq al- Urdun) was a former Ottoman territory incorporated into the British Mandate of Palestine in 1921 as an autonomous political division under as-Sayyid Abdullah bin al-Husayn. Transjordan was geographically equivalent to 1942–1965 Kingdom of Jordan (slightly different from today's borders), and remained under the nominal auspices of the League of Nations and British administration, until its independence in 1928. Transjordan became a kingdom and on May 25, 1946, the parliament of Transjordan proclaimed the emir king, and formally changed the name of the country from the Emirate of Transjordan to the Hashemite Kingdom of Transjordan. After capturing the 'West Bank' area of Cisjordan during the 1948–49 war with Israel, Abdullah took the title King of Jordan, and he officially changed the country's name to the Hashemite Kingdom of Jordan in April 1949. The following year he annexed the West Bank."
—Wikipedia

THE WATER WAR:

"In 1951 the tensions in the area were raised when, in the lake Huleh area (10 km from Banias), Israel initiated a project to drain the marsh land to bring 15,000 acres into cultivation. The project caused a conflict of interests between the Israeli government and the Palestinian Arab villages in the area.

(The) first summit of Arab Heads of State was convened in Cairo between January 13–17 1964, called by Nasser the Egyptian president, to discuss a common policy to confront Israel's national water carrier project which was nearing completion. The second Arab League summit conference voted on a plan which would have circumvent and frustrated it. The Arab and North African states chose to divert the Jordan headwaters rather than the use of direct military intervention. This led to military intervention from Israel, first with tank and artillery fire and then, as the Syrians shifted the works further southwards, with airstrikes.

On June 10th, 1967, the last day of the Six-Day War, Golani Brigade forces quickly invaded the village of Banias where a caliphate era Syrian fort stood. Eshkol's priority on the Syrian front was control of the water sources.

Problems can be seen to have emerged in 1999, when the treaty's limitations were revealed by events concerning water shortages in the Jordan basin. A reduced supply of water to Israel due to drought meant that, in turn, Israel which is responsible for providing water to Jordan, decreased its water provisions to the country, provoking a diplomatic disagreement between the two and bringing the water component of the treaty back into question."

—Wikipedia

www.ingramcontent.com/pod-product-compliance
Lightning Source LLC
Chambersburg PA
CBHW022153260626
47155CB00017B/1858

* 9 7 8 0 9 8 0 1 7 8 6 4 7 *